Uncle Morgan's Ghost

Books by Budd Westreich

THE DAY IT RAINED SIDNEYS

PLEASE STAND CLEAR OF THE APACHE ARROWS

UNCLE MORGAN'S GHOST

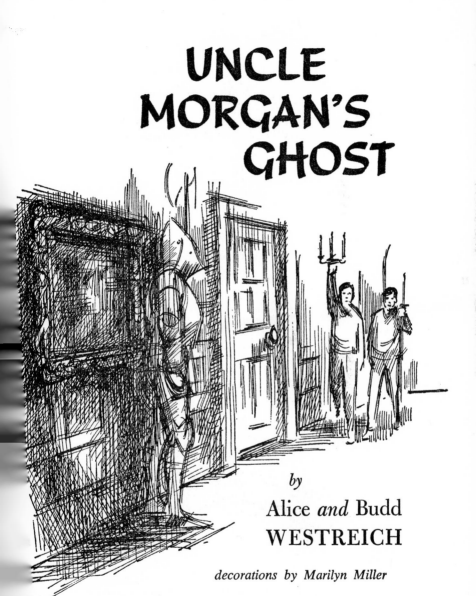

by

Alice *and* Budd
WESTREICH

decorations by Marilyn Miller

DAVID McKAY COMPANY, Inc.   NEW YORK

UNCLE MORGAN'S GHOST

LIBRARY OF CONGRESS CATALOG CARD NUMBER: 72-97807

MANUFACTURED IN THE UNITED STATES OF AMERICA

VAN REES PRESS • NEW YORK

Typography by Charles M. Todd

To Mother and Daddy,
George and Cecile

CONTENTS

Uncle Morgan's Ghost

1

The Shadow of Death

Beowolf the hound had been missing for some time when I arrived in England, Filbert Golightly was acting as if he was about to lose his mind, and Uncle Morgan's ghost was taking nightly strolls down the drafty corridors of Sudbury Hall scaring the pants off everybody.

I picked up this information shortly after arriving on English soil, and combined with the I-feel-sick pallor of Filbert's face, it was enough to start me thinking about taking the first available scow back across the Atlantic.

My name is Herb García. I'm an Indian from New Mexico (okay, so I'm only part Indian), and I didn't want to go to England in the first place. I was happy spending my summers digging for old bones in the sun-drenched desert I call home. I only made the trip because—well, see, I've got these two "rahther sophisticated" smart-alecky cousins in Albuquerque who've been leaping all over the world since they were twelve. And do they let me know it!

Every third word is, "Last year on the Grand Canal in Venice," or, "We saw this simply fascinating shop just off Piccadilly Circus in London." If I still don't look impressed

1

I'm liable to get hit with something like, "While strolling down the Ramplas in Barcelona last summer. . . ."

Me, I'm a real globe-trotter. I've crossed the bridge from El Paso, Texas to Juarez, Mexico—twice. And even for a high school senior in Pueblo, New Mexico, that's not doing very well.

In Stephen Potter's immortal words, "If you're not one up, you're one down." Cousin Philip and Cousin Flora were constantly one-upping me, and I decided that I just had to put an end to this "When we were climbing the Eiffel Tower" game. So during my senior year at Pueblo High I worked hard after school and on weekends and vacations and saved my wampum for a big summer "abroad."

That's how I got to England, and that's how I almost got a tomahawk in my noble redman's cranium (okay, so it's half noble redman, three-eighths Mexican, one-eighth Irish —and *all* American). It was all because of Filbert Golightly and his moldy Sudbury Hall.

Fil and I were old buddies. He had been an exchange student at Pueblo High during my sophomore year, and had lived at my house during his year in the U.S.A. And right there that says a lot about Filbert Golightly and raw English courage. Because during that entire year, he never once had a single nervous breakdown or even chewed one li'l ol' Anglo-Saxon fingernail despite the fact that my six little brothers and sisters constantly whooped and hollered around our house like the entire Apache Nation on the warpath. Even when my mom served him his first meal of *chili rellenos* with hot sauce, which must have seared the walls of his mild-mannered stomach tuned to nothing more explosive than roast beef and Yorkshire pudding, he just grinned and said, "Thank you very much, Mrs. García. Very tasty!"

I've seen stronger men come apart when attacked by those green chili peppers for the first time, but Fil stuck right with it. I guess that's why the English once got a toe-hold on so much of the world—sheer guts. By the end of the year I caught him eating those chili peppers right from the bottle.

So Fil and I got along fine, and my small tribe of brothers and sisters all fell in love with him and cried and shouted and hugged and kissed him when the year was up and he had to go home. I think that hugging and kissing part tore at him a lot worse than those first *chili rellenos.*

Anyway, Fil and I had great times together while he was with us and I guess he must have said a couple of hundred times that if I could come to England, I would simply have to stay with his family. So I did, and that's how I almost joined my ancestors in that great kiva (that's what you palefaces would call a Pueblo Indian church) in the sky.

After five pretty sea-sicky days on the Atlantic, I didn't feel or look too good when I was unloaded on the South-ampton docks. But I didn't look half as bad as Filbert. There was a hysterical look in his blue eyes that gave me the feeling that he was smack in the middle of a nightmare.

"Rough crossing, Herb, old boy?" he greeted me, when the customs men had finished searching my knapsack for smuggled automobiles.

"Not good, Fil ol' buddy. But what's happened to you? You look like you've spent the past week watching horror movies."

He winced at the word "horror." I guess it hit too close to home. Whatever was bothering him must have been powerful bad medicine, I thought at the time. He was a changed man. When he was running around New Mexico with me, he was like a spring that was wound too tight—always wanting to go here, see this, do that.

But the Filbert Golightly that greeted me at Southampton was a spring that had sprung. We left Southampton and had been driving for over an hour and he hadn't said more than five words, except to tell me that his parents were aboard a cruise ship on their way to visit relatives in Australia. Then he got frighteningly quiet, and he stayed that way.

I guess we Indian types are supposed to be stoic, but I take after my mother's side of the family—Latin and excitable. "Fil ol' buddy," I pleaded. "What's up? I've got the feeling you'd like to drive us off a cliff."

His eyes turned from the road and cut a couple of big holes in my face. "To put it succinctly," he said— nobody but Fil could spit out a word like "succinctly" and make it sound natural—"to put it succinctly, we've got a ghost."

"Doesn't everybody in England?"

Not a smile from him. "I know you, Herb," he answered. "You'll think this is a joke, something to make light of."

"Honest, if you tell me it's no joke, then by Geronimo, it's no joke. What's your ghost been doing?"

"Mostly killing pople," Fil told me, as if announcing the score of a rather dull cricket game.

Suddenly I had the feeling that England and New Mexicans don't mix well. So I closed the mouth and watched the rain, and there was plenty of it to watch. It rained all the way from Southampton to Sussex.

When we reached Sudbury Hall I felt worse than when I was unloaded off that tub in Southampton. No matter which way I looked, I saw it, and it was a horror. Towers and wings and bleak windows rambled in every direction. The gray stone walls and ramparts made sour faces at me, and

the ugly black sky settling down on the towers warned me
to get my soggy moccasins out of there while I could.

We drove alongside a high wall that ran forever, then
through huge ornamental iron gates onto a circular drive
that made a V at the immense front door of the manor
house. Just as we got to the gates, we passed a pedestal, on
top of which was a stone bust, a face from the past. I gave
it a quick once-over. From the look on its face, I don't
think that whoever it was or had been was too crazy about
Sudbury Hall either.

"Who's that, Fil?"

"That's our ghost, Herb. That's the founder of the firm,
you might say. Morgan, Fourth Earl of Sudbury. You'll be
running into replicas of him all over the Hall."

"Doesn't look like he was much of a laugher."

"I gather not. He was done in, you know. Murdered."

One thing about Fil, he could make the most terrifying
idea sound as commonplace as a weather report. Not me,
though. Words like "he was murdered" make me feel cold
and creepy.

"Now that you've explained," I said, "I can see why he
isn't laughing."

We stopped before the giant front doors and something
in a monkey suit came gliding out. He was too tall and
impossibly thin. I got the feeling that someone had put him
through the wringer on one of those old washing machines
and he had come out two-dimensional—that if he turned
sideways you wouldn't see him at all. A sickly yellow pall
under the wrinkles served as a complexion. This apparition
was Parkhurst, the butler.

He opened the door for me, all the time looking away as
if he detected an unpleasant odor in the air. He took my

knapsack and held it far from him, no doubt considering it the source of the offensive smell.

We entered Sudbury Hall. I wish I hadn't.

For the rest of the afternoon Fil did his best to work up a smile but never quite managed it. For a moment there I thought his gloom was going to crack, but then dusk settled in and a black sky smothered down over the ancestral home and he went ghastly again.

We were sitting in a football stadium called the Great Room, in thronelike velvety chairs that let you snuggle way down and then wouldn't let go. A coal fire glowed in a walk-in fireplace that resembled a whale's open mouth.

Fil stared numbly at a display of swords, knives, and spears arranged over the mouth—uh, fireplace.

The place was really making me feel vile. In self-defense I sent my mind back across the Atlantic to my home, warm and friendly, vibrating with the sounds of my noisy brothers and sisters. I thought of us all sitting together at dinner, hamming it up, safe and happy. And I thought of the desert under a bright, bright sun. Ah, the sunshine, that life-warming sunshine!

Then Fil brought me back into that mausoleum of a room. "That's what he's after," he moaned, looking up at the sword over the fireplace. "If only he would take it and go!" His hand made a fist.

"Filbert," I said, struggling to sit up in my red velvet chair. The sneaky thing wouldn't let go. "Old man, how about telling me the whole thing?"

At first I thought he hadn't heard me. Then he gave a small shrug and started talking in a steely voice that matched the cemetery atmosphere of the room. "Some months ago my father inherited Sudbury Hall. You know, Herb, that we were never wealthy, and so we were delighted when my father was located and told that he was heir to this place. Quite a fortune came with the Hall, even after the enormous inheritance taxes were taken care of. However, lately our joy has diminished considerably. There's something very much amiss here. It's almost as if the Hall is going to . . . do away with us."

"Oh, come on, Fil. You don't really believe that, do you?"

"None of us did," Fil answered. "My father still laughs at the idea, though, mind you, he doesn't discount the possibility of such things. My father's a most practical man of business. But the events of the past week or so since my parents left have convinced me that there are things present in this world that can't be explained. Things that are basically evil. Things that mean to harm us. Do you understand?"

No, I didn't. It was unlike Fearless Fil. "Easy now," I answered. "Just how is Sudbury Hall going to finish you off?"

"It's a legend, a very old legend. Ever since Morgan, Fourth Earl of Sudbury, was murdered, death has been waiting here at the Hall. I know that this sounds like a lot of nonsense to your American ears, but believe me, it's true."

I've heard some pretty tall tales in my time, but that story one-upped anything I'd ever heard before. "Where'd you find out about the legend? I take it your father hadn't been close to the rest of his family."

"When we moved in about four months ago, Mr. Walter Sage, who oversees the property, took my dad and me through the Hall. We found a strongbox that contained many heirlooms. One of them was a short history, written a hundred years after Morgan's death by Edmund, the Sixth Earl."

"What did good old Edmund have to say?"

"He writes of mysterious happenings at the Hall, and of death. Mr. Sage, who also laughed at the legend, told us that he'd known of these stories since he was a small boy. And his father before him, who also handled this Hall between tenants, knew of it. Sage says there are people in this county who swear that the stories are true."

"Exactly what legend are you talking about?"

"According to Edmund's history, the one that says when the hunting horn is heard, the ghost walks. And someone dies at Sudbury Hall."

"A horn?" I asked, still battling my chair. It was no use.

"It's a hunting horn. Shortly after it sounds, Morgan appears and walks the Hall, bringing the shadow of death with him."

I clutched my chest, fell back in a heap, and generally gave it away that I thought the story was fantastic. In fact I said, "Filbert, that's ludicrous!"

Filbert said, "The last time he came, he took Miss Stokes, a house guest. No trace of her was left."

So much for my brilliant opinions of the legend of Morgan's Ghost.

I couldn't top Fil's last statement, but I had a tough time making my ears believe what I had heard. Perhaps if I pumped some more information out of him, the fog would clear.

"Who was Miss Stokes?"

Fil sat up in his chair with ease and leaned toward me. I didn't even try to move. Obviously, my chair was stronger than his.

"There's a small cottage not far from here that belongs to

a retired Royal Air Force officer, Wing Commander Selkirk. Miss Stokes was the sister of one of his RAF chums. She came to visit him, and inasmuch as his bachelor's quarters were too small to adequately entertain a lady, he asked if I could have her here. As you can see, we have nothing but room."

"Looks to me like you could put up the entire Royal Air Force and still have room for a couple of Boy Scout troops."

Fil continued undaunted. He was used to me. "About three days after she came to the Hall, we heard the horn. It was late one night. In the morning she had vanished."

"Back up a minute. Is that all there is to the legend?"

"Perhaps some background would be helpful. You see, the Fourth Earl, Morgan, was killed with his sword while hunting—that's where the hunting horn figures in the legend. According to the writings we found, and the stories from the locals, the ghost of Morgan, Fourth Earl of Sudbury, keeps coming back to avenge his death."

"I can't really blame him," I put in. "If it had been me, I'd be furious."

Filbert as usual ignored me and pointed to the wicked looking sword above the fireplace. "That's the sword."

"But Fil," I protested, "you really don't believe all that stuff about ghosts! That's the kind of yarn I used to concoct to scare the *chicos*—the little ones. It's pure fantasy! We can't live on legends from the past—look what that has helped do to my father's people."

"I've heard the horn," Fil answered. His eyes became distant, as if he could see something I couldn't. "And I've seen the ghost of Morgan walking these very halls—a grotesque, glowing, angry Morgan." He was pale and shaking.

"You've seen the ghost!" I hollered, wishing I had six sets of eyes around my head.

Fil nodded. "He came along the hallway outside. When I entered the room I saw him trying to pull that very sword off the wall. I ran and switched on the lights. He simply vanished."

I wondered how long the cold chills would race around my short chubby body. "I don't want to hurt your feelings or anything, but could it be that you were a bit nervous, maybe a little shaky after hearing about that legend and you kind of *expected* to see him?"

I recognized Fil's rare impatient look. "I thought of that, of course. But when I saw Morgan the second time I knew it was real. That time he almost had the sword off the wall when I came in. In fact I heard it clinking some time before I reached the room. Once again, while I fumbled to switch on the lights, he vanished."

"Maybe you imagined it twice?" I squeaked. My voice wasn't convincing, and Fil was able to top that too.

"A witness was with me that time who also saw the ghost. Miss Stokes."

"The one who disappeared?"

"The same. That was the night she disappeared."

"I assume the police have been called in?"

"Come now, Herb," Fil said, as if he were talking to a child. "Certainly you know me well enough not to ask a question like that. Of course I notified the police, and at once. They have scoured the country, Wing Commander Selkirk has practically ruined his health looking, Mr. Sage has devoted weeks to the search, and Reggie and I have gone over the Hall itself at least a dozen times. Miss Stokes is simply not here. Or anywhere." His voice was beginning to rise with what might have been the beginning of hysteria.

"Hold it there, what's with this Reggie stuff? You're pulling my leg! I though Reggies only existed in old Saki stories."

Fil answered, "Reggie's my second cousin—my mother's cousin's son. He's . . . well, to put it in Yankee terms, he's a real oddball, but I think you'll like him. You know I've been studying music at the Fine Arts Academy in London." I well remembered Fil's skill on the keyboard. In fact, we set up a special assembly at Pueblo High just for his recital, and I'll tell you right now, those hallowed halls hadn't heard before or since piano playing like that. Fil's quite a pro, and our baby grand piano was one reason we were chosen to be his American hosts.

"Reg and I enrolled at the Academy together. He's a painter and sculptor, and he's rather good. He has no money, of course, and he needed a place to work. . . ."

"So you moved him right into Sudbury Hall. You're all heart, Filbert."

He looked embarrassed. "As I said, Reggie and I have been over this place again and again and we can't find a single clue to Miss Stokes's disappearance. And when Beowolf vanished—well, the ghost of Morgan, Fourth Earl of Sudbury, became very real indeed."

"You mean to tell me with your calm 'it's time for tea' English understatement that you had a Reggie and a Beowolf in the same house? No wonder you had troubles!"

"Beowolf is a dog, a big, lovely collie. We brought him with us when we moved in and gave him the run of the Hall. One morning he too simply vanished." Fil's reserve was close to crumbling. Miss Stokes had been his responsibility, and her disappearance had of course caused him deep and lasting chagrin. But Beowolf—Beowolf, it was obvious, was an old and beloved friend.

"Beowolf went *adiós* like Miss Stokes, huh?"

"Precisely."

"Couldn't he just have strayed?" I asked, grasping for a sensible explanation. "We had a collie once, and I know they're wanderers."

"Yes, they generally are, but Beowolf wasn't. Anyway, everyone in the county knew him. And we checked all around the manor. Inspector Wakefield, our local customs and excise agent, has a small spaniel. We thought perhaps Beowolf had called on the dog, but no one there had seen him."

"Are there many other houses or neighbors near here?"

"Not many. There's an inventor, Arthur Matlock, who's building some sort of jet engine in a garage about two miles from us. He boards at the Wakefield's, but he has no dog. And then there's Ben Richmond who lives down along the water. He has no dog either. That about sums up the local residents, unless you count a college student named Agatha Howe who has been staying farther afield at an inn called The Three Rams, and hiking over to do research on the area. We even checked with her. But she's seen neither Miss Stokes nor Beowolf." For a final touch Fil added, "And I know the police inquired much more thoroughly than I because they felt his disappearance could conceivably have some connection with that of Miss Stokes."

"Okay. You're telling me that you've seen the ghost of Morgan, Fourth Earl of Sudbury, twice. And that you've heard the hunting horn. And that a big collie named Beowolf and a grown woman named Miss Stokes have just vanished into thin air."

"That is precisely what I am telling you," Fil said, settling back in his chair.

"You know what, Filbert Golightly?" I asked, looking straight into his handsome face.

"What, Herb García?"

"I've listened to your story. I've carefully thought the matter over and after weighing all the evidence and examining and re-examining the facts, I've come to a conclusion."

"Do you care to tell me what that conclusion is?"

"I hate to break the news, ol' buddy, but it looks to me like you've got one heap of trouble here at Sudbury Hall."

2

Was That Beowolf?

We sat in the room for maybe half an hour, talking without saying much of anything. Fil stared at the darkening sky and I had a fit over the sound of my own breathing. Never sit almost alone in a silent, mammoth room; it does things to your nerve ends.

I had to think of something to keep from coming completely unglued, so I thought about what Fil had told me—an impossible story. But unfortunately, it was true. It had to be. Fil didn't lie. If he said that's the way it happened, then that's the way it happened.

Of course it couldn't have.

What I mean is, that's the way Fil *thought* he saw things happening. Now, what *really* had been going on at Sudbury Hall?

"Fil," I said, almost jumping out of my chair at the sound of my own voice crashing through the stillness and bouncing off the walls, "tell me some more about Sudbury Hall. Who lived here before you moved in?"

"No one, at least not for the past year. My father inherited the Hall from a great-uncle. Actually, I don't think my father had known of his existence. It took a year of legal work before Dad was declared heir to Sudbury Hall."

"So for a year the place was empty, right?"

"Yes, that's right, but where does that take us?" He looked over at me with interest.

"Don't look so encouraged, I'm still nowhere. I'm just trying to get some background about the place. While it was empty, who looked after it?"

"The local estate agent, Walter Sage. His family has lived in the county for a great many generations."

"Did he hear horns trumpeting and see ghosts?"

"He has never confessed to it."

"You mentioned some other people who live near here. For example, Wing Commander somebody."

"Wing Commander Selkirk. He's retired Royal Air Force. He's quite an expert on antique weapons and armor."

A spark was starting to burn upstairs. "Has he had a look at Uncle Morgan's sword over the fireplace?"

"He has indeed."

"And?"

"He estimates its worth as perhaps seven hundred pounds, or about seventeen hundred dollars. There are things of much greater worth in the Hall, if that's what you mean. It seems unlikely that a simple thief would concentrate on the sword."

"Oh," I said, a little depressed.

"The Wing Commander is coming to dinner tonight. In fact, so are several others. In your honor, old boy. I suppose it's jolly rude of me, but I've asked Parkhurst to make excuses for us until they've all arrived and dinner is ready to be served; I selfishly wanted more time alone with you. But you will get to meet the locals. You may pump them, as you say, as much as you like. I think you'll find them all quite civilized people with no ulterior motives or de-signs on this house or its possessions."

I would have given good odds right then and there that Filbert had just made his first big mistake.

I was about to throw another question when Fil shot from his chair, raced to the middle of the room and stood there in a most peculiar position, his head cocked to one side. Either, I thought, he had lost his marbles, or he was going to do a folk dance for me. Then I realized he was listening intensely.

"Do you hear it?" he whispered.

Poor guy, he's really lost his marbles, I thought. But I listened; I listened real hard.

Fil was now leaning on one foot with his hand cocked to his ear and his face in the pained expression of deep concentration.

"I hear it, I hear it!" he cried. "Don't you?"

So I listened some more. "Easy now, Fil ol' buddy. All I hear is the pitter patter of the rain and somebody's dog barking . . . somebody's dog barking!" I broke loose from the stranglehold of my chair. "You don't mean that's what's-his-name, your dog?"

"Beowolf! It's Beowolf, I'm sure of it! Come along!"

We went from the scary dry room into the soggy wet English air. I followed Fil out the side door and across a big spread of manicured lawn into the woods. I heard one more bark in the distance as we came out and that was that. I played follow the leader as Fil darted excitedly from tree to tree with his hands behind his ears and searched the grounds for a trace of his hound. I felt in my bones that that was the last bark we were going to hear from Beowolf. And it was.

"Oh, blast! He's gone." The light was poor, but Fil still strained to see.

I went over to him and put my arm around his shoulder. "Maybe it wasn't Beowolf. It could have been anyone's dog. Remember, you've been pretty keyed up lately."

Fil sagged. "I guess you're right. I don't know why I was so sure it was Beowolf. It's just that something inside of me said that it was. No, by Harry, I'd swear it was!" He shook his head and then looked hard into my face. "You did hear the barking, didn't you? I mean to say, my mind isn't slipping, is it?"

I had to smile. "Of course I heard the barking."

"But you've seen no trace of him since we came out?"

"Fil, this is one miserable place for a New Mexican to be holding a conversation." I put an open palm up to the sky. "I've had more rain fall on me in the last ten minutes than in about three rainy New Mexican years."

"Sorry, old boy," Fil said, and started back toward the manor. "I hoped to see something out here, that's all."

"I did see *something*," I confessed.

Fil stopped dead in his tracks and, with the rain running down his face, stared at me. "Are you pulling my leg, Herb?"

"Not out here, I wouldn't. I did see something. In fact, I still do. When I say 'now,' you turn around and look over there among the trees toward the back of the manor."

He stared at me. "Now!" I said. He turned in time to see the figure disappear farther into the trees.

"Why didn't you say something before?" Fil demanded, a little peevishly, I thought.

"What for? You were busy looking for your dog and she wasn't doing us any harm."

"You said 'she.' Did you get a good look? I couldn't tell who or what it was."

"I could," I answered soothingly as I cleverly tried to lead us out of the rain toward the house. He wanted to hear what I had to say, so he followed. Even in spite of the miserable rain, it took all the courage I could pump up to go back into moldy Sudbury Hall. Ugh, what a spooker!

"What makes you so sure it was a she?" he asked, right on my heels.

"Because, Fil ol' buddy, she's been watching us ever since we came out, and I've been watching her. While you've been galloping from tree to tree, so has she, keeping two big eyeballs right on us."

We reached the Hall and went in. "I don't know how you spotted her. I never even noticed, and I was looking."

"That's my father's genes coming out. I caught a glimpse of a brown suit and a red scarf out there just as soon as we left the house. Now, if my older brother Ramón were here, he would have *smelled* her from inside the house. You remember Ramón, don't you, Fil? He came home on his Christmas vacation that one time when you were staying with us. My big, silent brother, Ramón?"

"Certainly, Herb. I must say, he does look more of the noble Redman type I had envisioned in my mind's eye than the rest of the García family."

"Not only does he look Indian, Filbert, he *is* all Indian. Everything he inherited must have come from generations back. I'm not saying this because he's my brother, but believe me, Ramón is the most self-sufficient individual I've ever known. He was named for Mama's father, but he's never said much; he's just like Dad, the strong silent type. But there isn't anything he can't do. If you dropped Ramón on a barren, deserted island and came back a week later, you'd find him sitting by a blazing fire roasting a rabbit and with everything he'd need to survive for as long as he cared to stay there."

I'm not sure why I suddenly started babbling about Ramón. Maybe it's because I was scared and I missed him. Ramón is ten years older than me, and all my life he's been security for me, and for my brothers and sisters too, though he wasn't around as much for them. Whenever I got into a scrape, Ramón would suddenly and usually silently appear and get me out without so much as a word of reprimand, anger, or any kind of emotion that I could spot. He was long gone from home when Fil stayed with us; Fil had met him briefly that Christmas. Then he was gone again. Ramón. I liked to say his name.

We were in the house heading for the Great Room again. "Where is Ramón now?" Fil asked.

"I wish I knew for sure," I said, feeling wistful. "He's got a funny sort of job. See, he studied math and physics in college, and then he taught at a college for a couple of years. Everyone expected him to follow in Dad's footsteps and stay in education; I think Dad had secretly seen him as a college president or something. But then one day he showed up and said he was bored with his job and had decided to quit. He and Dad went into the other room to talk about it, and Dad got pretty upset. But no one could ever influence Ramón once he'd decided what he wanted to do.

"Ramón moved away from New Mexico to Washington, D.C., and since then we've gotten letters from him from all over the world. We never know where he's going to be until he's already been there, and I don't think we always know then."

"It sounds like he has an interesting job," Fil commented. "What precisely does he do?"

I wasn't sure why I found this such a ticklish question. Nobody had ever told me not to talk about Ramón's job, although nobody in the family *did* talk about it, around me anyway. But I didn't really know enough to hurt Ramón.

"He started out being a diplomatic courier for the State Department," I said, after hesitating a moment. "He went from country to country with his briefcase handcuffed to his wrist, delivering and picking up diplomatic papers."

I found myself unable to talk about it any more. Although Ramón and I were ten years apart, I had always felt close enough to him to be his twin. And for the past few years I hadn't been able to shake the nerve-wracking feeling that whatever his job was, it was no longer routine; that, on the contrary, it was often dangerous. I didn't believe he was still only a courier. He had too much on the ball not to have been tapped for more important things. I was secretly sure he was working in some way for the Central Intelligence Agency or some similar super-secret government agency. In my daydreams, I often saw him running, and wary.

But now a cheerier thought came to mind. "Hey, I meant to tell you! The last time we heard from him, he was in France, just across the English Channel. I wrote and told him I was going to be here and gave him your address, hoping he might be able to buzz over and see me. He said in his last letter he was taking a month's vacation. I hope it's all right with you if he stops off here?"

The look on Fil's face turned to one of delight. "My dear fellow, I should be relieved if he would! If anyone could help us get to the bottom of our mystery, I think he'd be just the man!"

"Of course I don't know if he's coming or not," I backtracked. "He didn't answer my letter, which isn't too unusual, but I'm not even sure that he got it. He might have moved on before it got there."

We sat back in our velvety chairs. Mine grabbed me as if it had been lonely while I was gone. The present caught up to me again. "I shouldn't have gone off about Ramón. Fil, listen, do you know who that woman was out there?"

"I'm afraid so. Did you see her clearly?"

"Well, let me put it this way. I wouldn't want to arm wrestle with her. She looked like she could throw both of us two out of three."

"That's our Agatha. Agatha Howe. She always wears a brown suit and red kerchief, as you described, and she has quite an athletic build."

"Like a small armored car. What's she doing here?"

Fil tapped his long fingers on the side of his chair. "That's a moot point. Debatable. She's the college student I told you about. She's doing research on the history of the county. We've all gotten used to seeing her stalking about, copying inscriptions off gravestones and sopping up the local legends."

"Is that what she was doing out there?"

"Most likely. Why else would a charming young girl be out in a storm, dashing about in my trees?" Fil said dryly.

I could think of a lot else, but I let the subject drop. I filed Agatha Howe away in my mind with the footnote, *try to avoid meeting her in a dark alley if she's angry.*

Fil began to pace. He hadn't believed his own explanation of why Agatha Howe was watching his house. Maybe he was still bothered about the barking. The more I thought of it, the more convinced I was that a man should know the sound of his own dog barking. But if the dog really was Beowolf, where had he been since he vanished? And why was he barking now? And why hadn't he come running to meet his master? And why had he suddenly stopped barking?

A look at Fil's face told me he was playing the same wondering game.

He stopped pacing and moved to the piano. The vibrations of mournful chords started drifting around the room. Fil's fingers were an extension of his mood, dark and apprehensive.

"That's a cheerful tune," I said pointedly.

He ignored me and kept on with the dirge. I shook loose from the chair and circled the piano. Then I spotted the tape recorder. "What's this for?"

He looked up to see what I was referring to. "Oh, the recorder. I use it to record my practice sessions. Then I play back what I've done and try to map out improvements. There's a national piano competition coming up in a few months and I had planned on giving it a bash. At least that was my plan before Morgan appeared."

We were back on that black subject again. So I pushed it a bit. "Just when did Morgan appear?" I asked as I slunk down on the piano bench beside him.

"When? Let's see. I suppose it was about ten days ago, shortly after my parents left for Australia." Fil changed to pensive chords. "Yes, it was just after Reggie found the diary."

"Uncle Morgan's diary?"

"None other. You see, Herb, shortly after we moved into the Hall, we decided to close off the east wing. It is much older than the rest of the place and in poor repair. It's directly on the river, and Reggie was pleased we were closing it because he thought it would be too damp for his health. He is delicate, you know. About two weeks ago, while I was out, Reggie went exploring in the east wing and found an old diary belonging to Morgan, Fourth Earl of Sudbury."

"He sure gets around, doesn't he?"

"Yes indeedy. As I was saying, the diary wasn't much, just odds and ends about what went on in the Hall in the late seventeen hundreds."

"That's it?"

"There was an interesting bit about a smuggler called Black Dan."

"Hi ho, I think I smell an olde English rat."

"He was that. Black Dan terrorized this part of the coast, smuggling and murdering at a great pace. He amassed fortunes. According to the diary, he forced Morgan into letting him use the Hall for hiding his contraband. Agents of the Crown were watching his movements and his normal warehousing facilities were closed to him. Naturally, Morgan was furious with Black Dan, but Dan had him in fear of his life. I recall one passage where Morgan wrote, 'Black Dan, the scoundrel, is storing his confounded booty in my Small Room. What joy it will give me to see that villain reap his just reward.' "

"A small room in this opera house?"

"I can't imagine what room he meant," Fil smiled. "But no matter."

Fil had piqued my curiosity. Black Dan sounded evil, but fascinating. "What happened to Smuggler Dan?" I asked.

"Hanged, of course."

"It figures."

"Shortly after he was hanged," Fil continued, "one of his men fell upon Morgan while Morgan was hunting and killed him with his own sword. Apparently he felt Morgan had been responsible for Dan's capture and hanging."

"It's a tidy story, anyway. Like an opera. Everyone has

quit breathing by the last act." A thought raced across my confused mind. "What happened to the diary?"

"Reggie has it about somewhere. It's of no great value to anyone but the family, if that's what your mercenary mind is dwelling upon."

It was. So Uncle Morgan's sword wasn't worth too much and his diary was in the same category. There went two very good reasons for someone to spook Sudbury Hall. The motive had to be more indirect.

"Who else knows about the papers Reggie found?" I asked.

"Just the whole county, those people in England who read the *Times,* and various other respectable citizens."

"Are you hinting that it was in all the papers?"

"It was in the *Times.*"

"And you've seen the spectral Morgan just since Reggie found the diary?"

"That's right."

"Aha!"

Fil looked hard at me. He was giving me a lashing with his blue eyes. "My dear Herb, this is nothing to be flippant about. The statistics cannot be disputed. When the ghost appears strange things happen at Sudbury Hall. Miss Stokes is gone. Beowolf is gone. According to the legend, when the horn sounds and the ghost appears, someone . . . always dies."

His voice trailed off to a tremble and his eyes grew wide and glazed as he stared around the darkened room. I saw his body stiffen, and he said tensely, "I can almost feel his presence in the room with us now."

We sat in the darkness in a maddening silence. The light was fading fast, too fast; I could barely make out Fil's face beside me. Everything was too tentative. I found myself peering hard into the shadowy outlines beyond the piano. The room seemed to be breathing, swaying in and out.

"This is ridiculous," I said to myself out loud. "Herb, get hold of yourself. You're letting this old manor house spook the pants off you. There are no such things as glowing ghosts and spirit hunting horns that sound in the night."

If I do say so, I was doing a pretty good job of mustering up my courage. I would have done even a better job, except that at that moment the hairs on the back of my neck stood straight up and my heart tried to thump its way out of my chest.

Fil froze as if a knife were sliding between his ribs.

Somewhere out in that murky forest that surrounded Sudbury Hall, a hunting horn was bleating a call; a call that seemed to suck the air from the room.

3

A Familiar Face

I shook so hard I almost fell out of my chair.

When I finally got my sobbing nerve ends back where they belonged, I raced to the window.

Fil came up behind me. "See anything?"

"No, it's too dark."

Fil nodded to himself and said in a voice as mournful as his music had been, "He'll come tonight. And someone will die! The shadow of death—it always follows the horn!"

"Cool it, Filbert," I said nastily. I guess I lost control of myself. I mean with a weirdo house, a crazy story about ghosts, and now a blaring hunting horn from the grave—boy! That house was getting to me.

We dragged ourselves back to our chairs and sat and made sour faces as if someone had poured sugar in the tank of our prize hot rod. For all the movement Fil made, he could have been as dead as Uncle Morgan.

Hey, cut that out, I told myself. Don't even think like that. Be logical, try to find something, anything, a clue, a reason. I was generating precious little, but I did get a glimmer.

"Fil, you awake?"

"Would that it were otherwise."

"Let's talk some more about that legend."

"Please, Herb, you've heard the story. You've heard the hunting horn. What else is there to say? Someone is doomed."

"Yeah, I've heard the horn, but this story is just too spooky for a desert rat from New Mexico to buy. You said you read about the legend in some kind of history, didn't you?"

"Just so. It was written by Edmund, the Sixth Earl."

"In his own handwriting?"

"Obviously, dear fellow, they had no typewriters in those days. The quill pen, remember?"

"Do I detect a wee note of sarcasm in that last line?"

Fil looked sharply at me, and then relaxed. "Sorry. As jiggly as I feel after that horn, it's a wonder we haven't come to blows. What about the legend?"

"Well, it's just that . . . suppose someone made up the story. Oh, I don't mean it hasn't been going from mouth to mouth in the county. We've got some pretty wild legends in my part of the world, too. But I mean, suppose that the Sixth Earl of Sudbury, Cousin Ed, didn't really write that history. Then it's just an old wives' tale and nothing more."

Fil looked disappointed, no doubt sorry I hadn't come up with something with more meat on it. "If that history is specious," he said, "if it really isn't the earl's writing, then perhaps you do have something."

I took a minute to figure out that "specious" meant "a darned lie" before I answered him. "What do you think? How genuine did it seem?"

"I think it's genuine," he said, his voice telling me I had

slid a doubt into his orderly mind. Where there's a doubt, well, maybe there's a clue.

He got to his feet. "I'll be back presently. I'll get the box with the documents."

He left me all alone in that nightmare of a room, and for the next five minutes I breathed slowly and listened hard enough to hear the squeak of a mouse with laryngitis.

Presently Fil came back. "Here's the box," he said, putting it down on the piano bench. He raised the dark carved lid and we looked at the beautifully handwritten documents. The one in question seemed authentic enough. I mean, the paper was old and antique-y looking and the writing was in big flourishes and swirls. I guess they wrote that way in those days. But still—

"Doesn't the ink look pretty solid to you, Fil?"

"Solid?"

"Well, just have a hard look at it. It's only faded a little bit. I'd guess that something written a couple of hundred years ago would have faded more than that."

"Hmmm. I should think you're right. But then the ink they used was remarkably permanent." Again I detected doubt sneaking into his voice.

"Fil, is there anything we could check it against?"

He started pacing. "Let me think."

Night had come to Sudbury Hall and we were doing our talking by the embers of a dying fire and a solitary yellow light from the lamp beside the piano. Fil walked back into the dark corners of the room. I lost him. Then his voice, with just a hint of life, came at me.

"I think I've got something," he said, coming back into the light. "Right here in this room, somewhere, there's a box of old letters. There might be one from Edmund. The collection goes back a great many years. Help me look; they're in a box similar to the one I just brought in."

We rummaged around the dark end of the Great Room. After a minute or two I grew accustomed to the weak light as we covered the wide bookcases built into the wall that seemed to go up a hundred feet. There were old books, some newer books, magazines, and, at last, two or three carved wooden boxes. Fil pulled them down and went to work.

I found what we were looking for. "This one's got a bunch of letters and some of them look awful old."

"Bring it over to the piano and let's have a look."

I put the box on the piano bench next to the first one Fil had brought in and we both started picking up letters and studying them. The third letter brought an ear-to-ear smile to my face. "You've found it?" Fil asked.

"I sure have. Take a look." I held it out to him. "See, it's signed 'Edmund.' But the writing is nothing like the writing on that history thing in the other box."

For the first time since I set my moccasins on that watery island, I saw real enthusiasm pop out all over Filbert Golightly. "You're absolutely correct, Herb. These two hand-writings aren't the same!" Then the life went as fast as it had come.

I couldn't have missed the disappointment oozing out of him. "Where'd I go wrong?" I asked.

"Good try, Herb, but wrong Edmund. This one wasn't the Sixth Earl of Sudbury."

I dived at the box and rummaged some more. "But this one was!" I held the letter up triumphantly. "And now, if you'll check the writing on this letter with the writing on the other papers, you'll find—"

"That the writing is identical. Sorry, old boy, but your

theory has just come apart. Here, let's compare the two more closely." We put them side by side on the piano and stared. The loops looped the same, the "i's" dotted the same, the slant and stroke seemed just the same. "No, Herb, sorry, but Edmund, the Sixth Earl of Sudbury, did write of the legend, so it's not just something an outsider made up conveniently."

I sank down in my chair and wanted to blubber. It had been such a nice theory. Why did it have to get blown to pieces? My spirits were low and weak enough to be picked up and carried off by an anemic ant. I didn't think I had a breath of excitement left.

But I did.

The hot breath on the back of my neck brought up a wild shriek that would have done my ancestors proud. I flew out of the chair and clawed at the air. When I came down, I heard a voice say, "Dinner is served, sir. The guests are assembled."

Parkhurst then vanished as mysteriously as he had appeared. I sagged over the piano and gave a pep talk to my heart.

Filbert put his arm on my shoulder. "Come along, Herbert. Some good English roast beef will soon put you right."

I followed. After a brisk hike we stopped before massive carved doors. They were so high I could have gone through standing on Fil's shoulders.

"What now, Fil?"

"Just be yourself." Then he thought about what he had said and changed his mind. "But do be careful about what you say to Reggie. He's still terribly upset about the disappearance of Miss Stokes and Beowolf."

We entered a long, narrow room with a high-timbered ceiling from which plummeted two huge twinkly chandeliers.

It wouldn't have surprised me to find bowling pins at the end of the table that extended almost the length of the room. At the near end sat a figure—I couldn't tell its sex from the wavy black hair—furiously feeding its face. Across from whoever or whatever it was sat two men, both looking intently at me.

Fil introduced me as the two stood. Walter Sage was a little butterball of a man with a shiny bald head. His jowls, his mouth, and his little blue eyes all smiled.

Wing Commander Evan Selkirk gave me a bob of greeting and a grunt and sat back down with ramrod stiffness on the first two inches of his chair.

Fil poked the chowhound. "This is Herb García, from America."

The glistening black hair fell back and I was surprised by a handsome, finely shaped face with curious brown eyes. The face grinned. The voice startled me. "A pleasure," Reggie said in a clipped Oxford accent.

Fil nodded and Parkhurst, moving like a hovercraft, wafted from the room.

"How are you feeling, Filbert?" the Wing Commander inquired stiffly.

"I really am quite fit, sir," Fil answered, as if saying his lines in a play.

"Splendid, splendid," the old officer responded, his mustache quivering slightly at both ends.

I wondered if I was supposed to have a script. I shifted about, casually put my hand out in front of me, and felt my fingers plop in a warm liquid. I glanced down to find a bowl of soup. It must have grown there; no one brought it and it wasn't there when I sat down. That sneaky Parkhurst!

For a time all was silent, except for the slurping of soup. Then Fil straightened and looked at Mr. Sage. "When you rang this morning you said someone had inquired about the Hall."

The little round man's jowls gave an affirmative nod before his thin lips spoke. "Yes, and rather odd, too. An estate agent from London rang up to tell me that he had a wealthy client who had expressed interest in the Hall."

"Pardon me," I put in, "but you mean that someone just called up and said he was interested and started asking questions?"

Walter Sage gave me a look as if maybe he thought I'd just arrived from the other side of the moon. "Not at all. The man was interested in purchasing it, of course."

Of course.

Fil showed no reaction. "Was any price mentioned?"

"Only a tentative figure, Filbert." The bald man grew confidential. "But it is twice what the Hall is worth, and in these days of inhuman taxes, you eventually must consider selling it, or at the least, turning it over to the National Trust."

Fil explained aside to me. "Many old families who cannot afford taxes on their familial estates turn them over to the government, the National Trust. That way, they don't have to pay the taxes, and the estates remain in their hands until they die, at which point the government takes them over and maintains them and runs tours through them."

Sage continued impatiently. "As I was saying, Filbert, there is, however, one condition our potential buyer made."

Fil kept spooning his soup. "Yes?"

I was going to butt in again, but I was still suffering from the wound Sage dealt me when I put my moccasin in my mouth before.

"Nothing must be removed from the Hall. He wants the

manor just as it is, furnishings, paintings, and so forth, all historically authentic."

"And I presume that means the weapons over the fireplace as well?" Fil said much too calmly.

Reggie's face came up. "Ghastly things, simply ghastly!" He shuddered, and fell back into his soup.

"Wing Commander," Fil called, "you have examined the armor and weapons in the Hall. Could there be anything extraordinary about them that we haven't noticed?"

"I doubt it very much, my boy. I've studied them rather carefully, don't you know. No, monetarily they're worth a good bit, but not enough to justify spending a hundred times their worth to buy the Hall."

"Then it simply doesn't make sense," Fil said thoughtfully.

Reggie looked up and his face showed he wasn't in the picture at all. "Whatever are you talking about, Filbert?"

Fil acted as interpreter. "The Wing Commander is making the point that if someone wants those weapons and armor in the Great Room, and it appears that at least one person does—" he looked at me to make the point that he was still convinced that the ghost of Morgan, Fourth Earl of Sudbury, was rattling around somewhere—"then it wouldn't make sense to offer a good price for the Hall to get them if they aren't worth very much."

"Quite right," said the Wing Commander.

I reached down to finish my soup. Only now it was roast beef. Parkhurst again.

The meal progressed in silence, and this bothered me. I just can't stand a roomful of people not saying anything. So I took another chance with Mr. Sage. "Fil tells me you're an expert on the local ghosts."

He didn't like the way I had put it. "I am familiar with the folklore of the area, yes. I have been managing and selling property in this county for a great many years. There are few establishments that I have not been connected with in one way or the other."

"That's what Fil told me," I said, trying hard to look charming. "But about the ghost. Can you tell me something about the smuggler, Black Dan?"

Again I had been too direct for our Mr. Sage. He stared at me, but answered. "I know many stories about that blackguard. He terrorized the entire county. Absolutely ruthless." The little bald head tilted back in thought. The flabby hands wobbled in my face. "You might find it difficult to believe the lengths to which he went. Once when agents of the Crown were after him, they posted a sentinel on the cliffs above the sea to watch for his ship. The sentinel placed white stones along the edge of the cliff to ensure his safety on dark nights."

All chewing in the room stopped. Everyone was looking anxiously at Walter Sage. "Dan heard of it and moved the stones."

"And the government man went over the edge," I put in.

"Precisely. But he caught hold of the cliff edge and hung on by his fingertips."

I could have guessed the end of the story, but Sage told it anyway.

"Black Dan ran out and stamped up and down on the poor wretch's fingers, crushing them until he let go and fell hundreds of feet to his death."

As I always figured, it was pretty tough making a living in those days.

When I finished my roast beef, I placed one hand on the edge of my plate. Parkhurst wasn't going to catch me napping this time. I waited, but the plate didn't move. I noticed that everyone was eating pudding. I panicked.

Looking down, I found a dish of pudding blinking up at me from beside my empty roast beef plate. Out of the corner of my eye I saw Parkhurst gliding into the woodwork. He was smirking.

"How are you enjoying your retirement, Wing Commander?" I called out.

"Oh, I keep myself busy. Perhaps Fil has told you that my hobby is collecting and cataloguing antique weapons and armor. Of course my pension is rather meager so I'm afraid I spend a great deal more time cataloguing than collecting."

"The quiet countryside doesn't bore you after an active career in the air force?"

The Wing Commander pointed a spoon at me for emphasis. "My lad, there's a time in life for everything. In my younger days the Royal Air Force was just my cup of tea. But now, in the autumn of my life, I'm quite content with the peace and quiet of the country. Every Englishman longs to live in the country, you know." I was taken aback to see the Wing Commander make an unpleasant face. "At least our countryside would be peaceful and quiet if it were not for that blasted Matlock."

Everyone seemed to understand but me. "I must have missed something, sir. How is Matlock changing the peace and quiet?"

I remembered Fil mentioning an inventor named Matlock living nearby.

The spoon was waving again. "With his blasted machine! It makes enough racket to be heard in Scotland. It shouldn't be allowed at all! Positively scandalous! He's a shocking fellow."

"You're quite right, Wing Commander," Sage agreed. "It's ruining property values in the entire county."

I was still in a fog. Fil helped me out. "Arthur Matlock is working on some kind of jet engine. Unfortunately, he works on it at night, and when he turns it on, as the Wing Commander said, it's enough to wake the dead." He paused, thinking no doubt of the dead Morgan. "There are times when it is so loud that it shakes the windows of the Hall."

That had to be loud, because those walls and windows were built for the ages.

I had to admit that the quiet countryside was ideal for testing an engine. As scattered as the populace was, he really couldn't do much harm, at least not to the human population. But I could see from the anger of Wing Commander Selkirk and the sympathy he was getting from Sage and Fil that the inventor was causing *someone* an inconvenience.

"How long does he intend to test this engine?" I asked.

"That's just the point, lad," the Wing Commander answered. "No one seems to know, not even Mr. Matlock!"

Sage and the Wing Commander commiserated with each other about Mr. Matlock and his foul machine. Fil was looking worriedly at Reggie, as if afraid that he would smother in his pudding. I felt like the sixth finger on a glove. I didn't belong there. I didn't know what was going on. I didn't like the set-up in Sudbury Hall at all.

And it didn't make things any easier to see a familiar face, peering in at us at the window.

4

Morgan, Fourth Earl of Sudbury

I didn't say a word. I didn't have to. Fil read my eyes.

"Whatever is wrong, Herb?"

"In this place, it could be anything, but let's put it this way. Are we all here—all the guests you invited for dinner?"

Now everybody looked at me as if I had lost my marbles. The Wing Commander, the roly-poly Mr. Sage, and even Reggie gave me the once-over and then cast their eyeballs on Fil, as if to ask if he were responsible for the strange behavior of his American friend.

"Are we the entire guest list?" Fil repeated. "Yes, we are."

"Well, our lady friend from this afternoon just arrived. She's peeking in at us at the window." Everyone turned to see. The face saw that everyone saw and vanished.

"Wasn't that the Agatha Howe you mentioned this afternoon?"

"That was Miss Howe," the Wing Commander said unhappily. "She's always snooping about, says she's doing a history of the county. Spotted her behind my cottage this morning. Most disconcerting."

"Why not invite her in?" I suggested.

"Jolly good idea," Fil answered, getting to his feet. "I'll see if she's still visible."

"Hold it, I've got a better idea. Send Parkhurst. The way he moves, he'd make the most skillful hunter look like a drunken elephant stumbling around in army boots."

Fil gave Parkhurst the word and the butler oozed out of the room. We waited, all eyes on the door. Two minutes, three minutes. In came Parkhurst escorting an attractive face with a no-nonsense short haircut and a body that wouldn't have done badly on the New York Jets.

"I do hope I'm not disturbing you," said Miss Howe, smiling as she came over to Fil.

Everyone seemed to know her and she gave each a little greeting. I was introduced and she bruised my hand as she pumped it up and down and announced, "A pleasure to meet you."

Parkhurst brought her some pudding and coffee. The air was strained in the room as she pulled out a chair beside me and put herself down with surprising grace. Agatha Howe may have been husky, but she moved like a panther.

"Out getting the air, were you, Miss Howe?" the Wing Commander challenged.

Miss Howe ignored the challenge and smiled with a certain charm. "I am sorry, gentlemen; it seems I'm rather potty about that. I mean coming up on people suddenly. I mean no harm, I assure you. It's just that I sometimes become so interested in my work—"

"Your work?" Reggie put in, brightening. "What sort of work do you do, Miss Howe?"

"Why, I thought you all knew," she answered. I must admit she had warm, disarming brown eyes. Maybe too disarming, I thought. "I'm doing graduate work at Bristol University, and my study is on the history of this county. So if you see me from time to time popping up here and there, take no notice."

"Perhaps I can help," Mr. Sage offered. "I'm interested in that sort of thing myself."

"That is what everyone has been telling me," she said, giving him another smile and widening the warm brown eyes. "I should very much like to meet with you and chat about some of the historic homes in this area. Of course this manor," she said with a wave of the arm around the room, "is most fascinating. I've been studying it diligently."

You mean you've been snooping around, I thought.

"Morgan, Fourth Earl of Sudbury, is one of the most interesting characters in the history of the county," Sage said, putting away a spoonful of pudding.

"I discovered that at once. There are likenesses of him everywhere."

You never knew what was going to set Reggie off. "Should have been bronzed," he said emphatically.

"Beg pardon?" the Wing Commander asked.

"Those busts of Morgan," our sculptor explained, "should have been bronzed, don't you think?" But he seemed to lose interest in Morgan, his statues, and the rest of us as his face disappeared back into his pudding.

"Was that you we saw this afternoon when the dog was barking, Miss Howe?" Fil asked, studying her with a calm but penetrating expression.

Miss Howe spooned some pudding and matter-of-factly answered, "You may have. I have been studying the manor today, but I don't recall a dog barking."

There went that word substitution game again. "Studying" for "snooping." It's amazing how a different word creates a completely different image. Who can argue with someone who is studying? Now snooping, that's not nice.

"How about horns?" I asked.

The big brown eyes went over me a couple of times. "Horns? I beg your pardon?"

"Just one horn, Miss Howe. Did you hear a hunting horn this afternoon?"

"Not that I recall."

Now Sage was excited. "You heard the horn, Filbert?"

Fil nodded. "I'm afraid so."

The chubby face grew agitated. "You must be careful."

"Have you discovered anything particularly interesting while 'studying' the Hall?" Fil asked the girl, ignoring Sage.

She thought for a moment. "Well, of course Black Dan is the most dramatic character I've come across."

Up went Reggie's face again. "Oh, I say, you've heard about Black Dan!"

"The history of this county *is* my field," she said with a hint of being insulted. "Obviously Black Dan would be known to me."

"Shocking chap," Reggie commented with enthusiasm.

Miss Howe threw the charm to Fil. "Actually, Mr. Golightly, I am rather a shy person. Perhaps that is why I try to remain in the background. You see, I have been trying to gather up my courage to ask for your help in writing my paper. I daresay you have old documents and papers that would be of great historical value relating to the manor and the history of the county."

This fullback of a female wanted something, all right. Even a country boy from the American desert could figure that out. So she wanted old documents about the manor, did she? Right there I was placing a heavy bet with myself that pure research wasn't the reason. What did this female, this picture of robust health want? Why was she snooping around, pardon me, I mean "studying" Sudbury Hall?

Fil was cooperative. So much so that I saw it irritated both Wing Commander Selkirk and Walter Sage, who hadn't taken their suspicious eyes off Miss Howe since she entered the room.

"I shall be happy to help you," Fil told her. "A bit later I'll show you some of the papers relating to the Hall and the family history."

Agatha Howe was thrilled. Sage and Selkirk threw Fil a look that said no, no.

Reggie could have been unconscious for all I knew. His hand had stopped spooning pudding to his face, so it was difficult to tell if he was alive at all, except that when I was beginning to worry, his face came up and he grinned. "Do excuse me, I must get back to work."

I sat there in the bowling alley of a room working on a headache. I sure had walked into something when I set my moccasins in Merrie Olde England. I was in mental quick-sand, going down slowly and surely.

But at that point, I didn't have the whole picture, not at all.

It was Parkhurst who broke the electric atmosphere of the room with an announcement: "Sir, Mr. Matlock is here asking to see you."

"Show him in, Parkhurst, and serve him some coffee, there's a good chap."

Now what would you expect if you were told that an inventor was about to enter the room? A frail figure, with long hair going in every direction over an absent-minded face, a soup-spotted suit, shoes that hadn't seen polish in months and maybe years. Right?

Wrong.

In bounded a smiling man in his mid-forties. He had a tanned face, white teeth and alert blue eyes. His blond hair was casually trimmed and he wore expensive slacks and sweater. Arthur Matlock struck me as more of a tennis or golf pro than an absent-minded inventor.

"Hi ho," he called with delight. Even the sour-faced Mr. Sage was forced to smile back. Mr. Matlock obviously knew how to handle difficult people. He was well aware of one of the most important rules of human relations—when you smile at someone, they've just got to smile back.

Fil motioned for him to sit down and he threw back a chair next to Mr. Sage and agreeably put himself into the picture. His easy manner siphoned off some of the suspicion charging around the room.

"Just thought I'd stop by and warn you," Matlock said lightly, after Fil had introduced me. "I shall be testing my engine tomorrow night."

"Decent of you to come by," Fil answered. "Frankly, Matlock, it's no inconvenience to me, but the sound does bother some residents."

Matlock was a sharpy; he caught on at once. "I do apologize," he said with sincerity to the Wing Commander and Mr. Sage. "I know it does make a dreadful row."

"It isn't that we want to stand in the way of progress, old boy," Wing Commander Selkirk said. "I spent a great deal of time in the RAF, and I know that it takes testing to come up with a new jet engine. But is there no way to muffle the sound? That blasted engine sounds as if it has enough power to break the speed of light!"

"Hardly that," Matlock smiled. "But I am sympathetic. I know it's a most shocking inconvenience."

"It's a jet engine you're working on, Mr. Matlock?" I asked.

"Call me Arthur, son, I know you Americans are informal. Yes, it is, a rather advanced design, I hope." In a good-natured way, he added, "You Yankees had taken the lead from us in aircraft advances, but along with other hardworking Britishers, I'm hoping to put the Union Jack solidly back in the picture."

I liked Arthur Matlock. He was a clever chap, because with that one statement he turned aside the wrath of everyone in the room. How could they be against a man who wanted to regain Britain's supremacy in the air? Especially an ex-RAF officer had to go along with him, even if his engine made enough racket to shake the foundation of Buckingham Palace.

Almost timidly, Mr. Sage asked, "Do you think you'll be at it much longer?"

Matlock threw up his hands in an I-wish-there-were-a-better-answer gesture. "I'm working just as fast as I safely can," he told us. "In this sort of work you never know when you're going to get a breakthrough. I do hope you understand."

"You really must have something," I remarked.

"I'm quite pleased with the progress I've made so far," Matlock told me. "My engine, when I get some of the rough edges smoothed out, should easily send a modern airliner on its way at over two thousand miles per hour. And it's a much lighter power plant than anything in use today."

If that was the case, I thought, he really had something. "That would be an aviation breakthrough," I said. "The little birds I learned to fly hardly make it over a hundred miles an hour with a good wind behind them."

"Oh, you fly then?" the Wing Commander asked, suddenly interested.

My answer made me a lot more acceptable in the eyes of

this old birdman. "I've got my license, and a few hours after that. But I'm still a long way from claiming that I fly. I kind of point the plane around the sky, and so far I've been able to walk away from all my landings."

"Good show!" the Wing Commander said. "It's a relief to see that the younger generation is interested in useful pursuits with some adventure in them. Sometimes I think our youth has lost its sense of challenge, of conquering our environment. All we seem to hear about nowadays from young people is their idiotic protests."

"Hmm," I said. I cast about for a way to put it diplomatically. "Maybe it's just that—well, we don't necessarily want to conquer the environment, sir," I said finally. "Some of us are concerned with learning to live in harmony with it instead. But, you know, most of my friends are too busy trying to get through school and find a decent place in the world to have time to protest. The loudest noise is being made by people trying to grab power for themselves. I don't think they represent all of us."

"Well said," Arthur Matlock put in. "It's time someone spoke up for the younger generation. Why don't you and Fil come by my shop tomorrow and I'll show you my machine. If you fly yourself, I think you'll understand its full potential."

"I'd like that, Mr. Matlock." I couldn't quite get "Arthur" out.

At this point the Wing Commander rose. "I must be going, and it is getting late. Call on me tomorrow, if you've time, Mr. García. I have a few antique items that might interest you." The fact that I could fly an airplane seemed to have made all the difference with the old boy. Here he was actually inviting me to his place, when at the start of the meal he'd hardly admitted I was in the room.

Sage left shortly afterwards, and Mr. Matlock, Fil, Agatha Howe, and I sat around sipping coffee and discussing the world situation, with no one saying anything that hadn't been said before. But one thing Matlock said did catch my attention. We had just been talking about the space achievements when he suddenly said to Fil, "What's been going on around here today? I was coming down the road when I heard the most awful row. Sounded like a dog had gotten his foot caught in a trap."

"We heard the dog, too," Fil said. "But when we went out to look for him, he was gone."

"Were you using a horn to call him?"

"Why do you ask that?" I asked, looking straight at his tanned face.

"Later when I was coming back from running some tests, I could have sworn I heard someone tooting a horn, you know, one of those horns for the hunt?"

Fil shook his head. "Sorry, Mr. Matlock, I can't explain that. Perhaps a child was passing through, playing with a horn."

Arthur Matlock said no more about it, and when he left, he again invited Fil and me to visit his workshop the next day. We told him we would and he went out into the night.

Fil, Agatha Howe, and I went into the Great Room, where Fil showed Agatha the letters and papers in the box. She went wild as she studied each document. "Oh, this is super! Would it be possible for me to come in again and copy these?"

Fil looked at me and then back at her. "I don't see why not, if they will help you with your paper."

"Oh, they will, indeed," she said excitedly. "I have some other papers relating to the Hall in my room at The Three

Rams. Perhaps you'd like to see them. They're just copies of originals that are in the British Museum in London. In fact, I have some letters from your ancestor, Morgan, Fourth Earl of Sudbury, and from later heirs to the manor."

"I say, I should like to see those," Fil told her.

I really couldn't tell what Fil thought about her.

When she had gone, Fil and I sat before the fire in the Great Room. Fil built the fire up, and I must admit it was cozier.

I was running over in my mind all that happened that evening. I don't know what Fil was thinking. After a long silence, restful and thoughtful, he got to his feet.

"Would you like to have a short tour of the house before we turn in?"

I liked the fire, and I was just getting accustomed to the Great Room. As far as I was concerned, the rest of the house was No Man's Land, dangerous territory. But before I could find some plausible excuse to beg off, we were in the hallway. There were no lights in the passageway, so Fil carried a candlestick. I felt like a character out of *Wuthering Heights*.

Off we went, down one hallway, into another, down another. We went through the Chinese, Indian, and Hunting Rooms, the this room and the that room, and all the time Fil was explaining about the men and women whose portraits adorned the walls. And in each room we found at least one painting or bust of Morgan, Fourth Earl of Sudbury.

I thought Fil was never going to run out of rooms.

As we approached the east wing, the air became foul with a raw edge that got inside you and slashed at your bones. Fil continued chatting about the history of the manor. I was tired, and frankly a little frightened. In spite of myself, I remembered the legend: when the hunting horn sounded, Morgan, Fourth Earl of Sudbury, walked the halls —and the shadow of death walked behind him.

I kept waiting for the right moment to suggest that maybe it was time to go night-night. But I couldn't find the appropriate pause to stick it in, so we plodded on.

Then I saw another image of Morgan, Fourth Earl of Sudbury, only it wasn't where it was supposed to be.

We had just made our way down a drafty hallway, and I was following my usual practice—usual since I arrived at Sudbury Hall—of looking over my shoulder.

"Look!" I yelled.

Midway down the hall behind us was a purplish, glowing figure in the costume of a cavalier. You know—cape, plumed hat, knickers and buckles. He was moving in an unnatural way.

It was none other than that fine old founder of the family line, Morgan, Fourth Earl of Sudbury.

5

Her Majesty the Queen's Customs Inspector

Uncle Morgan headed in the opposite direction, a streak of color.

"Hey, you!" I challenged. "Hold it, buddy! Friend!" He didn't stop.

Now here I must confess; I've been keeping something from you. When I told you that I was part Indian, I'll bet you imagined a tall, well-built athletic fellow with the speed of a jaguar, the power of a gorilla, and the silent wisdom of the owl.

Well, that's not entirely wrong. A few minor changes in the image, and it's one hundred per cent correct. Instead of tall, try short, about five foot seven. In place of well-built, slip in a nice sounding word like "stocky"—I'm a wee bit chubby. Never have a mother who's a good cook. Now the picture is perfect, save for one more small substitution for athletic. Here you might envision a good reader, because although I like just about any kind of sports, I've never been top man in this department. Now you got it, that's me.

Of course, if you really want to have the picture *perfectly* in focus, you might use "moves with the steady determination of a turtle" for "speed of a jaguar." As for wisdom, if you promise not to look at my permanent record card at Pueblo High, I'll promise not to look at yours. And the principal of Pueblo High is my father!

So. When Filbert Golightly came flying past me in hot pursuit of our spectral Uncle Morgan, it took a while for me to build up the steam to follow; which explains why that was the last look I had of Morgan, Fourth Earl of Sudbury, that night.

When I came trotting up to the door of the Great Room, Fil was standing there panting.

"Where's Uncle Morgan?" I asked.

"I almost caught him. He was standing there by the sword, glowing in the dark. When I dashed for the light switch, he vanished."

"Just like before."

"Just like before."

"Okay, where did he go?"

Fil looked somewhat annoyed. "I haven't the foggiest. For all I know, he could have vanished into the woodwork."

That didn't strike me as so impossible. "Maybe that's where he did go." I courageously charged into the Great Room. After all, Fil had already turned on the light.

Fil was really shook. He sank down into the clutch of his chair and complained, "It's impossible, it really is . . . he couldn't just vanish, poof, like that."

"Like I said, Filbert, I'm betting my wampum on the walls."

"Then you do believe in our ghost now," Fil said, eyebrows raised victoriously.

"He must have gone into the walls. I mean, a creepy old haunted place like this . . . I don't want to hurt your feelings, but I'll bet my last buffalo tusk that this place must be crawling with secret passages. As for believing in ghosts, maybe yes, maybe no. But I'm sure of one thing. The Morgan, Fourth Earl of Sudbury, that I saw hightailing it down the hall was no ghost."

"I won't dispute you, Herb. And perhaps there are hidden passages in the manor. I've thought of that, and I've banged my way around the walls in here and found nothing. Nevertheless, when you won't believe what you have just perceived with your own eyes, I surrender." He threw up his hands in disgust. I was real proud to have a friend who knew a word like "perceived."

We thumped around on the wall panels, turning every available knob, but came across nothing.

It had been a long, tiring day, the strangest day of my life, and as we left the Great Room, I was sure of something else. I wasn't going to sleep alone in a haunted room that night in Sudbury Hall. In fact, at that moment I was pretty convinced that I might not want to sleep with the light off ever again.

As we trundled up the huge curving staircase to the second floor, I said to Fil, "I hope you've got a nice bedroom somewhere big enough for both of us."

"I get your point. And I've already thought of it. With the shadow of death hanging over us. . . . Well, the horn sounded, and I'm not about to lose a friend tonight. There's a sizable sofa in my room."

If you cut off six feet from the length of Fil's bedroom, and shrink eight feet from the width, you'd just about have the size of the Pueblo High cafeteria. And the bed! The bed was something you wouldn't believe. Ever see a fourposter with posts ten feet high and a headboard with boars and elks plus two or three large herds of sheep grazing cut into it? I gaped and Fil grinned. "You take the bed and I'll sleep on the sofa." And because I couldn't resist the thought of telling my little brothers and sisters I slept there, I complied. I felt like a dinghy in the middle of the Atlantic.

Of course I knew I wouldn't get to sleep. Who could sleep in a haunted place like that? The horn had sounded, we had seen Uncle Morgan's ghost, and it was plain as the black hair on my head that good old Uncle M was due back to send someone off to the happy hunting ground. Right? No, *amigos,* not a wink of sleep for me that night!

When I opened my eyes, Fil said eight words that stirred me. "Hurry, Herb, you'll be late for breakfast." He was fully dressed, the sun was streaming in the long diamond-paned windows, and somehow or other I had lost a whole night. "Is anybody dead yet?" I asked.

Fil blinked. "Not yet, Herb. You needn't sound so eager."

It was a beautiful, glorious day and when I squinted outside at that golf course of a lawn, so green that it looked artificial, Sudbury Hall didn't seem quite so bad. In fact, all the nonsense about ghosts and horns blowing drifted to the back part of my mind, as if it had been just a bad dream.

Not only was the day beautiful, but Sudbury Hall was fantastic by the light of day. The antique furniture, the handcraftsmanship of an earlier day when people had time to put their personalities into their work, the warmth of the paneled walls, and the spaciousness of the rooms blended into an attractive picture of the past.

The sun really does make one heap of difference in how things appear to you. Maybe it's because I was brought up under its constant warmth and smile that I felt so desperate when I was without it.

Parkhurst served a solid breakfast. I doubted if he prepared it himself. There had to be a Mrs. Parkhurst some-where.

After breakfast, dressed in my best formal wear, faded Levis with matching jacket, I joined Fil on a tour of the grounds.

We had been over the vast manicured lawn and through the forest the day before. They looked a lot better today. Bless you, sun.

"What's at the end of this forest?" I asked as we poked along.

"The river. Be careful, the ground just drops off at the edge of the woods, and if you are not expecting it, you're liable to go off yourself."

The trees just stopped and so did the ground. I gazed down at a small river maybe fifty feet below us. "How do we get down?"

"There's a safe path. This way."

We wound down to the swift little river. Even on the banks, the constant patter of English rain had its effect; things were growing everywhere. Bushes and trees hung over and into the river hiding the banks. It was a pleasant scene.

I felt so good soaking in that sunshine that my mind wasn't thinking of much. "You know, Fil, it's like a different world down here, so quiet and protected from everything."

"I know, I come here quite a bit myself when I want to be alone and think."

"I can see that by your footprints," I remarked pointing down at the ground as I sauntered along. "They are yours, aren't they?"

"How could that be?" Fil answered. He was making a big fuss over a simple remark, I thought. Then he put his shoe next to the footprint on the ground. "Bad guess," I admitted. "They're not yours, then."

"No," Fil answered thoughtfully. "But who could have been down here? The Parkhursts never muck about outside."

I gave the footprint a hard, hunter's look. "I know. It's probably the Amazon's. Agatha Howe."

"Maybe," Fil muttered, keeping his eyes to the ground now as if he had lost a pocketful of change. "Look, here are more footprints, and these are different."

So they were. "Maybe Agatha has a boyfriend," I suggested.

Bad suggestion.

At that point I wasn't as mystified about the footprints by the river as I might have been. I had just a hint of an idea why they were there. As to whose feet they came from, well, I could only guess. I had a last look at the river winding gracefully in the sunlight with lush green foliage growing over and into its cooling water, and then Fil and I went back up the path toward the house.

"I think it's time you met the rest of the cast of characters in this neighborhood, as you Yankees say. Come on, let's pay our customs inspector a visit. But don't be alarmed if he insists on searching you."

That last statement set up an image of Inspector Julius Wakefield as a suspicious, don't-trust-anyone representative of Her Majesty the Queen's customs and revenue department.

"How far is his place?" I asked as we walked along the country road boarded by the high wall of Sudbury Hall.

"About two miles. The walk will do you good."

"I'm not complaining, Filbert ol' buddy. You know, this dripping country of yours is absolutely fantastic when the sun shines."

"I'm glad you think so. I don't think an Englishman ever finds anyplace as beautiful as his own country ... in the spring, I admit. There's a famous poem that goes, 'Oh, to be in England, now that April's there.' "

We moved to the side as a truck came up behind us and then drew alongside and stopped.

Fil smiled at the driver. "Can I be of assistance?"

"I hope you can," the driver said, leaning over. "I'm looking for the office of an estate agent name Sage, Walter Sage. Do you know him?"

"Continue on the road for another mile and then turn to the left. It will take you to the village and Mr. Sage's office."

"Thanks, mate."

"I wonder why that truck was going to Sage's," I mused out loud.

"In these parts," Fil told me, "just about everyone who has any interest at all in buying and selling property deals through Walter Sage. His family has been here for centuries, and is quite well known and respected."

"We must be near the sea," I said after a short walk. "I can smell it!"

"You desert dwellers have good noses," Fil teased, "and you're quite right. Around the next turn you'll see it."

I sped up. I love my desert home, but there's something about the sea that goes through me. It's so, so ... well, alive and exciting. And it smells of distant places and three-masted schooners heeled over chasing the wind. My insides get all zippy when the soft scent of the sea reaches my nostrils. Feeling a little idiotic, I took off running. Around the turn and there it was, blue and inviting. And there, out there, a freighter silently moved on a blanket of rippling blue toward some exotic port. Okay, so it was probably a coaler going to fill its belly with dirty, smelly coal from some equally dirty, smelly port. Can't I wax romantic for just a bit?

But back to Filbert and me and our trip to see the customs man. I learned something that day, about things going on along the south coast of England, that shouldn't have been. And any day that you pick up even one little bit of stuff you didn't know, that's a day well spent.

Inspector Wakefield's cottage must have been modeled from a storybook; you know, the peaceful vine-covered cottage set among trees beside a sapphire sea. It was white with leaded windows and a real thatched roof. In the sunlight its white sides were dazzling, contrasting against the azure water.

The picture was so magnificent I came to an abrupt stop and stared, drinking in the scene, and felt a sudden surge of emotional recognition. In the back of my mind I heard myself saying, "Someday, I'd like a place like that."

"Are you feeling all right, Herb?" Fil asked, coming up beside me. "You look—well, odd."

"Forget it. Let's meet Her Majesty's customs inspector."

The inspector must have leaped from the same storybook as his house. He was pruning roses in the garden, dressed as if he were about to step to the bridge of a transatlantic liner and guide her through the briny deep. He saw us approaching and waved with one gloved hand while the other held a pair of clippers. Even at a distance his blue navy jacket with the gold braid, his nautical cap, also with braid, his white shirt and black tie set him off as a man who was proud of his service.

But what really set him apart from other men was his beard, a magnificent, well-trimmed red beard that said straight out, here was a man who was as much a part of the seascape as the gulls soaring and diving among the waves.

His smile and his handshake were warm and reassuring. I was introduced and knew that the inspector was sincerely happy to meet a stranger. But in that moment of greeting I was also very sure that here was a man I didn't want as an enemy.

"Come in, lads, come in," he said, putting down his clippers.

"Are you going out today?" Fil asked, pointing to the uniform.

The inspector laughed and his mouth and eyes made one of the handsomest smiles I've ever seen.

"If you mean do I usually do my gardening in my uniform, Filbert, the answer is no. We are going out this afternoon to test the *Dorset*. We had some modifications made to the engine and I want to make sure everything is in first class condition before we make our duty run this evening."

"Is that the name of your ship, the *Dorset*?" I asked as we came into a large, comfortable room with rugged beams and knickknacks befitting a man of the sea. A brass ship's lantern stood in the middle of a table. Anchors, fishing nets, a ship's wheel, and various other nautical things, the names of which I don't know, except that they belong on ships (even in New Mexico we get to watch sea stories on TV) were tastefully placed about the room. In fact it seemed odd that we weren't rolling and pitching. Odd, but fortunate, because my stomach had proved itself to be a poor sailor on my recent trip across the Atlantic.

"The *Dorset* is our cutter," the inspector explained, motioning for us to sit down. Mrs. Wakefield, a plump, motherly looking woman, came in with some lemonade. She and the inspector looked very much at home with each other, as if in addition to being man and wife, they were good friends. Again I was introduced.

From where I sat I had a spectacular view out the window to the sea.

"How are you enjoying your stay?" the inspector asked.

"Last night the word 'enjoying' wouldn't have been appropriate, inspector," I said bluntly, "but right now, sitting in this marvelous room in this fantastic house, looking at the view out this window, I'd say I'm enjoying it just fine."

I think my frankness startled Fil, but the inspector laughed. "You speak your mind, don't you, son? I admire that." He turned to Fil. "But I have heard that you've been having trouble at the Hall."

"That we have, inspector. Of course you know about Miss Stokes and Beowolf. Last night we heard the horn again and—" Here, Fil got embarrassed, so I filled in for him.

"And we saw the ghost."

"That's what I heard."

"You did?" Again Fil was startled.

"That's my job, son, to know what goes on along this south coast. Mr. Matlock told me," he explained, pointing to the ceiling.

"Oh, he's renting a room from you?" I asked, surprised.

"Yes, and a very good tenant he is, too," the inspector commented. "Quiet and well-mannered. The wife and I haven't a complaint in the world against him. But his infernal machine, well, that's something else again. There are many times when I'm not pleased that my job takes me away from home at night. Tonight I'll count my blessings. But even ten miles down the coast we'll be hearing it."

"You go out at night, sir?" I asked.

"That's one of the hazards of my trade, son. Most smugglers are fools, or they wouldn't be in that line, but they are not foolish enough to try to unload anything on this coast unnoticed in the daylight."

"Makes sense," I said.

The word "smugglers" was exciting in itself. It conjured up pictures of adventure, secret coves, ships moving stealthily through the fog. And after I thought about it a bit, it painted other more realistic pictures of handcuffs, courtrooms, and prison bars. As I looked across the table at Inspector Wakefield, I decided that anyone trying to get contraband onto his part of the coast better be ready to spend a long vacation in Her Majesty's jails.

"You must know this part of the landscape pretty well," I said.

"I confess that I do, Mr. García. Every cove and inlet and landing for many miles in either direction."

"Then I guess it's safe to assume that not much contraband is getting through these days."

It was my time to be startled. Inspector Wakefield's handsome face was now not so pleasant. Even his beard seemed unhappy. "I wish that were true, my lad. I wish that were true."

6

Fire!

The customs man was wounded, not physically, but inside, where it hurt a lot more. One look at him told you that he had pride, pride in his work, pride in his ability to keep his part of the coast free of smuggled goods. And now his face showed that he had failed. I wished I hadn't brought up the subject.

"There has always been a lot of smuggling along this coast," Inspector Wakefield said. "It would be impossible to cover every inlet, cove and landing place from here down to Land's End and up the east coast to Margate. But we do our best." He shrugged, wrinkling his neatly pressed blue officer's jacket. "Lately, our best has not been good enough."

"I didn't realize that," Fil put in. "Is it organized, inspector, or just the casual small boat owner coming back from France with a few odd bottles of wine and such."

"I'm afraid it is a good deal more serious than just the odd bottle of wine, Filbert. We have had reports from London that goods of all kinds have been appearing about the country, goods that did not pass customs on their way in. And every lead points back to this area."

I stared out the window at the blue sea and my eye was caught by the wake of a large speedboat making lazy circles across the gentle waves. It was as if the owner were trying to perfect his skill in handling the craft. First there were circles and then figure eights. The pilot was obviously skillful.

"Is it really that easy to sneak past you at night?" I asked, and then I wished I hadn't said that either. No point in rubbing salt in the wound.

But he laughed. "I wouldn't have thought so, Mr. García. Until recently I thought we were very efficient. We have a fine craft, fast and silent when we want it to be, and a good, dedicated crew to man her. But lately, someone has found a way to skip past us, as you have pointed out."

I took a long drink of my lemonade. Very good. "I assume you don't publish where you're going each night in advance."

"Hardly. Each evening, about an hour before we go on patrol, my crew meets right here in this room and we decide where we'll go that night. Frankly, I usually don't know myself which area we'll patrol until everyone is assembled here."

"Why do you wait until the last minute?" Fil asked.

"I suppose it is because I am basically a cautious sort, Filbert. If I plan our patrol early in the day, there is the possibility that I just might say something inadvertently to someone and give away our plans. If I don't know myself just where we are going until we are about to leave, there is no danger of such an unfortunate error."

I tried to visualize the scene in my still somewhat fogged mind. The amount of smuggled goods was increasing and the authorities felt they were being brought in near here. The inspector's job was to stop the smugglers, but they were apparently getting past him. He had a fast ship, a good crew, and no one knew where they were going until just before they raised anchor. Yet someone was still slipping past them. Impossible!

"Have you any theories, inspector?" I asked. "Because what you have just told us doesn't seem to make much sense. It's obvious that you're good at your job. Why should things suddenly go bad?"

"Lad, I would like to have sixpence for every minute I've pondered that little mystery."

"How about someone coming in by air?" Fil asked. That was just what I was thinking.

"It's possible, but where would they land?" the inspector answered. He also had given that idea quite a bit of thought. "There are no airfields nearby, and while you can muffle the engine of a small boat, there's not much you can do about the sound of an airplane going overhead. Someone would surely have heard it. And lads," the handsome face with the seafaring red beard looked thoughtfully at us, "whatever goes up—"

"Must come down," I finished. Then I glanced idly back out the window, hoping to see some more maneuvers of the big speedboat. But it was gone. The ringing of the phone in another part of the house brought my attention back to the room.

It was time for us to leave, and as I was about to catch Fil's eyes so we could make our excuses, Mrs. Wakefield hurried back into the room. This time she wasn't carrying lemonade and she didn't look at all motherly.

"Julius, get down to the dock straightaway," she said in an even voice. "The *Dorset* is on fire."

There went a perfectly peaceful morning, shot. I had no time to give the matter much thought because after "Come along, lads, we may need extra hands," we were out the door following the inspector down a path that led to the sea.

It was all downhill and I had to pull back as I ran so I wouldn't go over on my head. After about a hundred yards of trees we came to a short level stretch and our path became a dock.

The inspector was far ahead of us, Fil was close behind him, and I was behind Fil, by how much I'd rather not say. They both disappeared inside a sleek cruiser that I guessed to be perhaps forty feet long.

Smoke was curling up from a hatchway at the stern. I thought it best to wait on the dock. So I did and then I noticed that the *Dorset* wasn't the only craft tied up. Farther down the dock was the speedboat I had watched from the inspector's house.

Inspector Wakefield, Fil, and a sailor came on deck. They chatted for a while and then the sailor went below and the other two joined me on the dock.

"How bad was the fire, inspector?" I asked.

"Dame Fortune was with us, Mr. García. One of my crew was sleeping below and the smoke woke him. He was able to put it out at once."

"You don't have to be very careless to get a fire going," I said. "Even on the desert where there isn't much to burn, careless campers will start the sage on fire."

I was facing two very intent eyes. "This wasn't carelessness, lad," Inspector Wakefield intoned. "Someone tried to set our engine room afire. We had a bit of luck because at this time of day there usually isn't anyone on the *Dorset*. My engineer had some work to do on the engine and came down early. Otherwise there wouldn't have been anyone aboard her at all and she would have blown up."

Well, here was one job you couldn't pin on Uncle Morgan's ghost. If he did it, he was sure a long way from home. Now someone *real* wanted the *Dorset* out of action. Who?

The next fellow in the scene gave us a clue. Trotting down the dock toward us came a chap I guessed to be in his mid-thirties, with longish black hair, a turtleneck sweater and soft, casual leather shoes.

"I saw the smoke and rang your house straightaway," he panted as he came to a halt in front of us. "Is she all right, inspector?" He seemed genuinely concerned.

"No damage, Ben. One of my crew was aboard and put her out before she could do much harm. That smoke makes it look worse than it is. We should be able to go out tonight," the inspector answered. Then he remembered us.

"You know Filbert Golightly, don't you? This is his friend, Herb García, from America."

We shook hands and it was a pleasant change to shake hands with someone on the same level. At that point I didn't know just where Ben Richmond stood in this tangle of weird happenings, but he had one thing in his favor as far as I was concerned; he was my size. And that was very good, because I get tired of having to look up to people while I'm pumping their paws.

Ben had one of those animated faces that showed every thought in his head as he thought it. As he chatted with us we saw concern, some fear, perhaps for the safety of the crew of the *Dorset,* and finally wonder and bewilderment. "How did the bloody thing get started?" he asked. "Someone careless?"

I didn't know how Inspector Wakefield was going to answer that. Did he trust Ben? "Not carelessness at all," the customs man answered candidly. "Someone tried to set her afire. Did you see anyone about, Ben?"

You could see the fellow thinking, hard. "Let me see. I was out practicing with my speedboat." So he was the skillful pilot I had seen maneuvering over the waves. "I brought her in and went up to my cottage to write down an idea I had before I forgot it. And then I saw the woman."

"What woman?" Fil and I asked together.

"I'm not really sure, chaps. My cottage is quite a distance up the hill. I was at my writing desk which faces the sea and I saw a woman come out from the trees and move toward the dock. That's all I saw because my view of the dock is partially blocked by some trees. However," and here he seemed to be thinking hard, "I got the impression it was the same rather odd girl who always seems to be wandering about the woods lately. You know, the college student staying at The Three Rams."

"Miss Howe?" Fil asked, as if he couldn't believe it.

"Yes, that's the one."

"Are you sure it was she?" Inspector Wakefield asked.

"I didn't really see her face, but she was wearing that same red kerchief and brown suit that Miss Howe always wears."

That was Agatha Howe. Had she set the *Dorset* afire? I didn't know much about English schools, but it struck me as a pretty weird requirement for doing a paper on the history of the county. If at this point you're getting the idea that maybe Agatha Howe wasn't all she said she was, I confess I had the same nagging suspicion. Then who was she? And why had she tried to burn the *Dorset*?

We said good-by to the inspector and started back up the hill toward the road. Ben Richmond walked beside us, still looking upset. He seemed genuine enough, but one thing puzzled me. He had said that he had gone up to his cottage to write something down before he forgot it.

I have a hard time keeping what's in my head out of my mouth, and I asked, "What was it you were afraid you might forget, Mr. Richmond?"

"Pardon?" Then he was with us. "My work. I'm a writer."

"What kind of stuff do you write?" I asked as we started up the path that wound up the hill.

"Mysteries. I had an idea for a plot and I didn't want to lose it."

"Sounds exciting. Do you write about a lot of different characters or do you have the same one in all your books, like Agatha Christie's Hercule Poirot?"

Ben Richmond's face said he was puzzled. Maybe he was still thinking about the fire on the *Dorset* and Agatha Howe's strange appearance on the dock. Then again, he might not have heard me, because although we Americans and English are supposed to speak the same language, I had already learned that we don't. "I like reading about the same character," I said. "I'm quite a mystery fan. Do you use the same character, you know, like John Dickson Carr's Perry Mason?"

"No, I try to create a new set of characters for each book." He smiled at me, taking no notice of the hard look I gave him. "Nice to meet another mystery buff, even from across the ocean."

Ben took a turnoff in the path that went up to his cottage and Fil and I climbed past the inspector's place up to the road. We had a magnificent view of the coast as we followed the highway. We were going away from Sudbury Hall.

"Where to now, Filbert?" I asked as we wound around cliffs that overlooked the sea. Ahead, the road descended and ran beside the waves.

"Remember, Wing Commander Selkirk asked us to stop by. Maybe things will be a little quieter at his place. You know, my friend, you're having a pretty exciting vacation, aren't you?"

"I could live without the excitement. Your Sudbury Hall caper is like putting together a five-thousand-piece jigsaw puzzle."

"No puzzle at all," Fil protested. "You simply refuse to believe what has unfolded before you. I can tell that by the way your handsome face makes little editorial comments when something happens."

"And what does that mean?" I felt suddenly naked.

"It means that when you don't like what is going on, it shows on your face. It also shows when you're suspicious, like when we were chatting with Ben Richmond."

"Now you're going to make me self-conscious."

"About your face?"

"If it gives away my feelings, yes. And also I always feel funny when someone is continually watching me."

We must have gone ten feet before my last remark penetrated. Fil started to slow down. I said very softly, "No, keep going."

"What did you mean by that remark about someone continually watching you? You certainly don't think anyone has been watching you since you came to England?"

"Take a quick look at the trees on the other side of the road."

Fil looked. "You're right again, Herb."

7

With Reggie for a Friend, Do We Need an Enemy?

"What's wrong with that kooky female?" I said, watching the unmistakable red kerchief disappear behind some trees.

Fil kept watching the trees as if he thought she might reappear. She didn't. "I don't know, Herb. At first, I thought she was, well, just a bit odd. We English have our types, and we try to be tolerant of everyone, no matter how strange they might appear. However, this is too much!"

"You mean her following us?"

"That doesn't bother me," Fil said, taking long, angry strides along the road. "But if she set fire to the *Dorset*, it stretches the limits of anyone's understanding."

It sure did, and it also raised some more questions. The answers were painfully obvious. Who set fire to the *Dorset*? Why, Agatha Howe, of course. There was a witness, or at least *almost* a witness. Ben Richmond didn't really see her strike the match, but who else could have done it? She was the only one around. The answer came too easily, and I didn't feel comfortable with it.

The sun remained high and bright and our view as we descended down the winding road to the sea was fantastic. I don't think I've ever seen anything so beautiful. Now we were walking almost level with the blue waters of the English Channel. We crossed a small bridge where the land parted briefly, making a quiet inlet that poked farther into the land to our left than I could see. On the other side of the bridge, which was an arched stone structure that must have been put there many hundreds of years ago, a narrow paved road joined the main highway.

"This is it, Herb," Fil said starting to turn. "This road follows along this little bay to the Wing Commander's place."

I think he was about to say something else, but he didn't because at that moment a car came from behind us and a cheery voice called, "Morning, fellows. Having a good walk?"

We turned together to see a black Rover zip past, going on toward the village. Someone was waving at us. Someone with a pretty face, and a red kerchief around her neck. Agatha Howe.

I waved back and smiled. Fil was too upset. "She certainly has a nerve," he said, more to himself than to me. "First she trails us like a hunter stalking game, and then she comes flying by, all smiles, as if we hadn't noticed her antics. I think she's crackers."

"I guess she must have gotten tired of playing huntress and managed to hitch a ride," I speculated.

We followed the narrow road away from the beach. The trees grew thicker and although we were right beside the little inlet, or bay, as Fil called it, in many places the foliage was so thick we couldn't see through it.

"What's that?" I asked as we came to a low ramshackle

building standing about ten feet back from the water. It had no windows and no doors that I could see from the road.

"Just a deserted boathouse," Fil answered, as if to say, "What else could it be standing right there by the water?"

"Let's have a look."

"But the Wing Commander's cottage is just ahead," Fil protested.

"It won't take but a minute." I left the road and scooted down a small rise of land that led to the beach. My first impression was correct. The building had no windows. But I was wrong about the doors. As I came around the front I saw them, huge double doors with a large padlock. For a ramshackle building, it was well built, because I couldn't even find a loose board to peek in.

Fil was annoyed to be wasting time there. I didn't keep him long. "I guess when the tide comes in it reaches these doors."

Fil studied the quiet waters of the inlet and then looked at the doors. "Now, that is strange. No, I don't think the waters come up that far." He studied the ground and then grinned. "Here's the explanation. See the tire tracks in the wet sand? They use a boat trailer to get to the water." There were two parallel tracks in the sand, very wide apart.

"Must be a wide trailer," I commented.

"Well, take a look at the boathouse. It's very wide. Must be a good-sized craft." I realized that Fil was getting impatient, so I led the way back toward the road.

Wing Commander Selkirk's cottage sat back about fifty feet from the peaceful waters of the inlet. I learned from Fil that its style was popularly called Tudor, after a period of English history. Pure charm. It was a low cottage with a sloping roof, and was built of white stucco spaced with wide brown boards that ran up and down all around, with an occasional brown board running sideways.

It was the kind of picturesque little cottage you'd like to put in your pocket and take home. If the Wing Commander had any close neighbors, we couldn't see them. The cottage seemed to be sitting all alone, in a quiet woods, with the front windows looking out on the inlet.

"I wondered if you were going to come," the Wing Commander greeted, throwing open the door as we approached. "Delighted that you could make it. You're in time for lunch." When standing, Wing Commander Selkirk was as ramrod as when seated. I got the feeling it would have been impossible to even imagine the words *slouch, sloppy,* or *casual* when thinking about the ex-RAF officer. I guess his clothes were supposed to be casual, an open shirt and slacks for working, but on him they became formal. He motioned for us to come inside and then moved into the house to continue doing something with his hand.

When we came into the house I saw what he was doing with his hand. He was taping a small piece of gauze over a raw, red splotch on the back of it. The small table by the window held a tube of ointment, which at first I mistook for some kind of suntan lotion.

"I'm afraid old age is making me clumsy," he explained, putting the finishing touches on his bandage. It was as neat and correct as everything else about him. "I was doing a spot of gardening and wasn't properly attentive. Rose bushes are lovely, but their thorns can be nasty business. Sit down, chaps. Delighted you could come."

The Wing Commander's cottage was small, but snug and relaxing. While the furniture was old, it was inviting. You know, stuffed chairs with plump pillows. Even the wooden chairs, which were old and aristocratic, were carefully designed for people to enjoy sitting in them. I could have guessed what would be on the walls before I entered the room. And I would have guessed right. Airplanes, pictures of airplanes of every kind and description. There were many from the First World War; some biplanes, with one wing above the other, and some triplanes, with three wings stacked on top of each other. And between the pictures of airplanes were photos of men in uniform. Beneath their pictures were personal messages: *To my old comrade. . . . Best wishes to an old friend,* and so on. The dates said that many of these birdmen had been long gone.

We sat down at a round table dominated by a row of books in the center, held there by two solid book ends, each in its neat place. You guessed it, more airplanes. Only jet fighters this time. And each book end plane was flying toward the other one with some fifteen books, all about flying and aircraft, between the two. The only other things on the table were some papers which I'm sure made no sense to Fil, but which were familiar to me. As part of your training to receive a private pilot's license you must go to ground school and learn, among other things, meteorology, which means weather. A pilot who doesn't understand weather isn't going to be a pilot very long, because it's weather, and not the airplane malfunctioning, that causes most crashes. Although these reports were slightly different from the sequence weather reports I had studied to get my private flying license, the information was the same. The Wing Commander noticed my interest.

"Ah yes, Mr. García, you did tell me you were qualified to fly. Then you will understand those weather reports."

"They're not like the ones I'm used to, Wing Commander, but I think I can read them."

"Capital, capital, my boy. As you can see, even after

thirty years I find it difficult to get flying out of my system. Only now I do it in my imagination. Even a grounded bird can keep its thoughts in the sky."

"You must have had an exciting career," Fil put in. I know he must have felt somewhat out of the conversation since he was not a flier.

"Indeed it was, Filbert," the Wing Commander answered, his voice full of nostalgia.

"What kind of aircraft did you fly?" I asked.

"Just about every kind that came along." He chuckled. "My most exciting moments were in flimsy craft that are no longer around today, except perhaps in the antique aircraft museums. Ah, that was a different day for the airman. No weather reports in those days! You flew by instinct, held up in the clouds by glue, canvas and bits of wire. But, by God, you flew!"

"Were you flying in the Second World War?" I asked.

"Certainly, but even in those long gone days, I was a little old for the fighters. I would have given a year's pay to fly one of the Spitfires. Instead, I was with air rescue, piloting small flying boats up and down this coast, picking up downed airmen." His voice was still back in the past. "Those flying boats may not have been Spitfires, but that was flying too, and a tricky time we had of it."

Wing Commander Selkirk came quickly back to the present, a bit embarrassed that he had let his mind wander back to happier days. "We're not keeping you from anything, are we?" I asked, trying to cover an awkward moment.

"Not at all, lads. In fact, I am frankly delighted to have some company. Why, look at the time! You will stay for lunch, won't you?"

The Wing Commander whipped up a very nice lunch. I didn't recognize the meat in the sandwiches but it was good.

There were also some sandwiches which I was sure held nothing but cucumbers, and I was surprised to find that they were very tasty. The tea was strong and hot.

It was a pleasant lunch and I enjoyed Selkirk's company and hearing his stories of his early days in the Royal Air Force. He may have been a grounded bird, as he put it, but he certainly had had his day. It was daring men such as he who had taken flying through its pioneer, trial and error days. And I knew that many of his friends staring at us from the walls had paid the full penalty for the mistakes made in the beginning days of flying.

It was early in the afternoon when we left the cottage among the trees and started back for the main road.

"I feel sorry for the old boy," Fil said as we trudged along. "A quiet little cottage on the south coast must be quite a comedown from his adventures in the clouds."

"I'm sure it is, but there's a time in life for everything. And now is his time to retire and take it easy. He has his memories."

"I suppose that's more than many people have at his age."

"Say, you told me he was a collector of antique weapons. I didn't see many around, just an old sword and some flint-lock muskets on the wall."

Fil turned to me, his blue eyes confidential. "I didn't mention the weapons and antique armor, Herb, because he doesn't have much left."

"What do you mean, *left*?"

"I heard that when he first went into retirement a few years back, he had quite a collection. But his pension is small, and living costs, even in that quiet cottage, are high. And he does enjoy a vacation on the Continent in the winter. He has had to sell a piece from time to time. I'm sure he would have been embarrassed if I'd said anything about it."

"You're a bit stuffy, Filbert Golightly," I said, "but you've got a good heart."

We reached the main highway with its magnificent view of the English Channel. "Are we going back to the Hall?"

"It's still quite early, and it is such a lovely afternoon," Fil said, stopping. "You haven't seen our fair little village yet. Are you game for another short walk?"

"Why not?"

So we headed down the highway, moving farther away from Sudbury Hall. I liked that. My insides kept repeating that Sudbury Hall was not all that crazy about me. But despite the hocus-pocus, the ghosts, and the hunting horns that signaled death, I thought I was beginning to understand what all the confusion was about.

The village was just that—small, tidy, and ready to be photographed for a picture postcard. As was true of most everything else I had seen on that south coast, it might have been put up exclusively for the tourist trade. It seemed unlikely that such picturesque, quaint and charming houses, countryside, and the village itself had just grown there like cities, towns, and houses grow in other parts of the world.

The village bordered the sea. The first building you saw, because it was the first one you came to and also because it was the largest structure, was The Three Rams Inn. It too was Tudor and quaint. In front of the building, swinging in the slight sea breeze, was a neat and colorful sign showing three rams with curly backswept horns. Beyond it were three small, equally attractive buildings.

The first one beyond The Three Rams had a neat and dignified sign on the window, WALTER SAGE, ESTATE AGENT. Fil led the way in.

Our chubby Mr. Sage was busy with a customer, pointing to something on a large wall map, which I guessed to be of the county. The man was nodding and answering back in a low voice.

We waited and when the man left, Walter Sage noticed us and beamed a greeting.

We shook hands. Then Sage assumed a concerned expression. "Heard about that nasty business with the *Dorset* this morning." He shook his head disgustedly. "What is the world coming to when a young girl tries to destroy a ship?"

"Then you've heard the whole story?" I asked.

He nodded, and his eyes met mine as he explained. "This is a small place, Mr. García. News, particularly bad news, travels fast." He turned to Fil. "Is the inspector going to press charges against Miss Howe?"

"I don't see how he can, Mr. Sage. After all, no one really saw her do any damage."

"But she is the most likely suspect, isn't she?" he asked, more as a statement of fact than a question.

"I suppose she is."

"Strange girl. What can she be up to?" Then another thought struck him. "I have found someone who has expressed great interest in the antique weapons and armor at Sudbury Hall," he announced cheerfully. "And I think you can get a very handsome price for them, too."

What? Someone else interested in Uncle Morgan's sword? What would Uncle Morgan say? Fil and I were equally startled by this announcement, and I'm sure Fil was about to say "Nothing doing" when the front door opened and Sage said in a hushed voice, "This is the man now, Mr. Cravatt. I told him to come back and see me and I would find out if you were willing to sell. How convenient that you are here."

"Are you engaged?" the man said, hesitating at the door.

"Not at all. This is young Mr. Golightly, whose father owns the Hall. Perhaps you would like to repeat your proposition to him."

Mr. Cravatt was a mousy man with a syrupy smile. He made about three running bows as he came at us. "How fortunate you are here! I was telling Mr. Sage earlier today that I was interested in your collection. I'm a dealer."

I didn't think that gooey smile could get any gooier. It did.

"That's what Mr. Sage has been telling us," Fil responded.

"Would it be possible for me to examine the collection?" the man asked, rubbing his hands together in anticipation.

Fil thought for a minute and then said, "No, not at the moment, Mr. Cravatt. After all, the Hall doesn't belong to me. My father will be back in a few weeks and then I shall inquire if he is interested in selling the collection. There's really no point in having you go to the trouble of looking it over if my father isn't interested in selling."

"It's no trouble, at all, dear boy."

"I should still rather wait," Fil answered, firmly.

Cravatt was disappointed and his smile, for just one second, slipped. "In the event that the situation changes, you will contact me, won't you?" he asked.

"I promise," Fil answered.

"Mr. Sage knows where to reach me." Cravatt gave a little bow and scurried to the front door.

"He has an unfortunate manner, that one," Mr. Sage said, "but he is one of the most reputable dealers in the business. He can probably make a handsome offer for your collection, Fil."

"For my dad's collection."

"Quite right, Filbert. But keep it in mind."

I didn't say much until we were back in the street and then maybe I said too much. "What's with all this traffic around Uncle Morgan's moldy old swords and knives, Fil? And that Mr. Cravatt is oily enough to shimmy through the inside of a drainpipe."

"I quite agree. There definitely is too much attention being paid to Uncle Morgan's sword, as you so charmingly call it. And I'm quite sure Wing Commander Selkirk's estimate of its value is accurate. There must be something else about that sword."

"Something you don't know and someone else does," I said. But Fil was intently gazing back toward The Three Rams. "Is anything wrong, Fil?"

"Oh, sorry," he answered. "It's just that I saw Reggie going into The Three Rams."

"What's so startling about that?"

"Nothing, really. Only he so seldom leaves the Hall. I wonder why he's here? Let's have a look, shall we?"

As we came alongside the dining room of The Three Rams Inn, I glanced in and saw Reggie stop by a table and put down two packages. Then he looked around, as if searching for a waiter. I grabbed Fil's arm and kept him from going in the door.

"Why are we stopping?"

"Take a look in the window."

Fil gave me a quizzical look, shrugged, and stared into the restaurant. "Why, he's chatting with Miss Howe. How strange! I didn't think he cared for her at all."

I stared too. Miss Howe was leading Reggie out of the restaurant. They were deep in conversation.

"Maybe he has taken a fancy to her. If not for the fact that she's a bit on the husky side, she's an attractive girl."

"I don't deny that," Fil answered. "But I know Reggie

usually tries to avoid her. And look, he's left his packages on the table. Perhaps we should go in and keep an eye on them for him."

So we did. Inside we sat at Reggie's table and waited for our long-haired genius to return. Fil was frowning and troubled.

My attention was drawn to the two packages. "I'll bet I can explain this. Fil. He probably came into town to get some artist's supplies, you know, paints and plaster for sculpting. Should I take a look?"

"I shouldn't think he'd mind."

I pulled back an edge of the paper covering the box. I didn't need to see any more. I grinned. It isn't often that I'm right. "Sure enough, Fil, this is a box of artist's colors."

"And the other package?"

"Probably more of the same," I answered. "But it's a weird looking package." Brown paper had been casually wrapped around something with a curve. I pulled back a bit of it and gaped for a long time before I dared speak.

"Well," Fil demanded, scorching me with his look, "what is it?"

"You won't believe me if I tell you."

"Don't be a fool, Herb. What's under that brown paper?"

I gulped, took a deep breath and answered, "A horn, Filbert ol' buddy, a hunting horn."

8

The Infernal Machine

For the longest minute that I can remember, Filbert Golightly just stared. He was flabbergasted, and terribly hurt. He had trusted his cousin from childhood, and now—if one jumped to conclusions, a pretty easy thing to do with that hunting horn staring up at us from the table—it meant that our artist friend was stabbing his newly rich relative in the back.

After a long moment of reflection, Fil decided not to make the leap. At least he was ready to have some doubts and give his cousin a chance to explain.

"Let's leave, Herb," he said softly. "I haven't the faintest idea what Reggie is up to, but I think it best if we wait before we condemn him."

"I'll go along with you there," I answered, getting to my feet. I didn't say more; it would only have hurt Fil. But what was Reggie doing with that horn? And also, what was his connection with Agatha Howe?

We were back in the street. I hesitated, not knowing which way to go. Fil had made his mind up about something. "I know this is a terrible thing to do," he apologized, leading me across the street.

"You're trying to tell me in your delicate English prose that we're going to hang around for a while, see what Reggie does, and follow him."

He got that impatient look again. "Crude, but accurate. I can't take the suspense."

We waited beside a building where we could take a peek now and then and see what was happening at The Three Rams. And as we waited, my mind tried to make connections. I had the feeling that we had our hands on a great many links. Now I had to put them together to make the chain. Where did Reggie fit?

"How did you happen to invite him to the Hall, Fil?"

"Now look here, Herb, I know you mean well, but your tone implies that you think Reggie had some sinister motive for taking up my offer to move in to Sudbury Hall. That's ridiculous! He didn't angle for an invitation and was startled when I asked him."

"Could he have developed that sinister motive, as you put it, since he came to the Hall?"

Fil snorted.

"How about that hunting horn?"

I had him. "All right, Herb. Perhaps that isn't quite so ridiculous. But he may have a perfectly reasonable explanation for having it."

Fil was trying so hard to convince me that Reggie was a number one fellow, trusted friend and relative, that I knew he wanted to reassure himself. It would have hurt him more if I pushed the point, so I let it drop there and we waited. I'm not so sensitive. Reggie seemed likable enough, but I didn't really know him. Life in my part of the world is less sophisticated and people tend to move with deliberation, with a good reason for everything they do. Despite the polish and sophistication of England, I didn't believe people behaved very differently. Reggie had a hunting horn. Reggie seemed to be buddies with Agatha Howe, a rather strange girl, and a likely suspect to say the least.

Presently out came Reggie, his hair hiding all of his handsome face. Under each arm he carried a package. Off he went on the road toward Sudbury Hall, and we were behind him. Fil looked terrible. My Indian blood started to bubble. We were stalking game in the best tradition of my forefathers.

Was Reggie going to meet someone? Or was he going to deliver the horn to an accomplice? Keep after him.

"You're obviously enjoying yourself," Fil said, a little resentfully, I thought.

"There is a little thrill of the chase in this," I admitted.

We followed Reggie away from the village, up the hill, beyond the cutoff road that led to the Wing Commander's place. Some of the thrill of the chase pooped out. I think we could have been five feet behind him and he would never have noticed us. His hair sheltered him from the world and the world from him. And he kept going, straight and steady, not looking this way or that. He must be a deep thinker, I said to myself. How can he ignore all this magnificent scenery, and above all, us? If he glanced back he'd spot us. But he didn't. Wherever Reggie was headed, he was going there with determination.

To our left, small boats were sailing and motoring in the calm sea. After a while I quit staring so hard at Reggie, and drank in the scenery. A beautiful red and white catamaran zoomed past, and farther away from the shore, motorboats were making their way along the coast.

It was a typical, summer scene along the south coast. The

only thing odd about it was us. We were following Reggie as if he were an evil agent for a foreign government. After a half hour of that very dull chase I was beginning to feel a bit foolish. Here in this quiet, normal summer scene, we were playing Sherlock Holmes and Doctor Watson. And making a mess of it.

But then I realized that something unusual was happening. Fil spotted my suspicion as if he had just noticed a hunting dog raise its nose to pick up a scent.

"What now, Herb?"

I gave him my best grin. "Okay. Everything looks quiet and peaceful, right?"

Fil glanced around, in front at Reggie stalking determinedly ahead, and behind at the empty road, and then to the trees. "You're not going to tell me there's someone in those trees again, watching us?" he asked, keeping his eyes glued there as if he expected that to be just what I did mean.

"Not this time. Listen to the sound of the motorboats. Notice how they get louder as they come up to us and quieter as they move away from us?"

"Quite normal, I should say."

"Without looking out at the water, listen now, Fil. Is there a different sound out there?"

Fil walked a bit and listened and then nodded. "I believe you're right. The sound of one motor stays at the same volume, as if the boat were keeping to a steady speed. Do you think it's *following* us?"

"I think Reggie is the quarry and not us. They've come even with us, but they've never gone beyond us to Reggie. Whose boat is it? Do you know?"

Fil took a quick look. "It's Ben Richmond's." He shook his head despondently. "Good Lord, Herb, this is really getting to me. It was difficult enough when all I had was a simple ghost. I was learning to live with that. But this is beyond me, simply beyond me." His voice trailed off and there was pain on his face.

"Easy now, pal. Don't let all this zippity-do spook you. There's more to this game than meets the eye. Come on, we're falling behind. I think Reggie is simply going back to Sudbury Hall, but let's make sure."

Reggie turned in at the huge iron gate and we watched him thread his way along the road toward the house.

"Shall we go in, too, Fil?"

"You've seen just about everything of interest today, except one. And as it is still light, let's complete the tour." Fil led me down the road alongside the high stone walls, away from the manor.

"And what's of interest here?"

"Arthur Matlock and his 'infernal machine,' as the Wing Commander calls it. I don't know much about flying or jet engines, but inasmuch as you are a member of the flying fraternity, you might enjoy it. Anyway, Mr. Matlock will probably be offended if we don't call today."

We walked for fifteen minutes and crossed one of those picturesque stone bridges that arched over a small river. From the way it curved away, I assumed this was the same little river that ran behind Sudbury Hall, the one overgrown with foliage that Fil and I had explored earlier that day. The one with the footprints we couldn't explain.

Once across the bridge, we turned left and followed a dirt road, hemmed in with grass and bushes, that was headed the short distance to the sea. Arthur Matlock's laboratory was a large, wooden shed placed just short of the English Channel in a pleasant grove of trees beside the mouth of that small river. It was here, behind his building, that the sweet water of the river met the salty English Channel.

Fil paused at the open doorway, and then hearing hammering inside, walked in.

Arthur Matlock was not as nattily dressed as he had been the previous night. He was in a greasy pair of what had once been white coveralls, fighting a battle with a huge, somewhat battered jet engine that was up on mammoth blocks of wood.

He grabbed a rag and rubbed his hands as he greeted us. "Well, chaps, I was wondering if you were going to make it today. What do you think, Herb," he said to me (very informal for an Englishman), "ever seen the likes of her?"

He was proud of his—whatever it was. So I played the game. "Boy, that certainly is a jet engine!" I exclaimed. I couldn't miss there. Whatever else it was, it was a jet engine.

"Thought you might appreciate it," Matlock said, beaming. "As you may have noticed, it is quite conventional, but I've got some electronic hookups that will act as a turbocharger and supercompress the air, doubling the horsepower. At least I hope it will work out that way. Take a look."

He led us to the front part of the engine where a great many strange wires and connections and "things" that I didn't recognize hugged the round jet engine. He could have told me that the contraption made milkshakes and I wouldn't have argued with him. Technical material at that level is way over my head. Fil tried to show his enthusiasm with an empty grin. He kept shaking his head as Matlock explained his wonder. Arthur Matlock read the response as it was intended.

"I can see that you fellows have some appreciation for machinery," he complimented. "Unfortunately all the local folk don't seem to feel the same way. That Wing Commander, for example. Stuffy old bird if I ever saw one. Don't get me wrong, chaps. I admit, when Phoebe gets warmed up, she can bring up the bodies in a graveyard, but after all, where would the world be if we let a little noise stop progress?"

I was tempted to say "Better off" but swallowed it. I didn't want to be around when he flipped the switch, which I remembered was to be that night.

"We certainly wish you all the best of luck, Mr. Matlock," Fil said. I'm sure he was thinking the same thing I was. Let's get out of here before this thing goes off!

"Arthur, please," Matlock corrected. "Now what have you chaps been doing for fun today?"

"Well, we stopped by Inspector Wakefield's earlier today. You weren't there or we'd have said hello," I said.

"Sorry, but I've been at work on Phoebe all day. It's comfy at the inspector's for me, you know. I've got a lovely upstairs room overlooking the sea and Mrs. Wakefield must be the best cook in the county. I'm going to be sorry to leave those comfortable lodgings when my work is finished here. Was the inspector puttering in his garden as usual? He's bunkers about his plants."

"He was when we got there," I said, "but the fire took care of his gardening."

Matlock became suddenly alarmed. "What fire? Not that lovely cottage!"

I was sorry I had opened my big mouth. Fil came to my rescue.

"Nothing to worry about, Mr. Matlock, I mean, Arthur. There was an accident aboard the *Dorset*. Just a lot of smoke. We all went down and had a look and everything is fine."

I thought that this might be the right moment to say bye-bye, but then the phone rang. "Excuse me, chaps," Matlock said. "I've been waiting for some parts to come down from London. That must be what this call is about, at least I hope so. Hang on, this shouldn't take long."

He went off into another room and we heard him chatting with someone.

"What do you think of his engine?" Fil asked, when Matlock was out of the room.

"Well, he seems dedicated enough. But I'm no expert on jets. It just might do what he claims it will do. After all, the first jet engine was made in this country by Commodore Whittle. Everyone at that time must have thought he was an eccentric too."

Matlock was back. "Everything's in order. The parts will be here in a day or so." Then he grew businesslike. "I'll be giving Phoebe a good test run tonight. If you like, you could come down and watch."

"Well, er, I think we have some plans this evening at the manor," I fumbled. "Don't we, Fil?"

He picked it right up. "Yes, we do. Terribly sorry, Arthur, we certainly appreciate your offer. Perhaps some other time."

"I'll hold you to that," he answered. "And I'm very relieved no damage was done to the engine of the *Dorset.* She's a fine ship and I know how attached Inspector Wakefield is to her. I know what it means to have affection for a machine," he added, patting his engine as if she were a prize hound.

He went back to work and we went out the door, stumbling through the disarray of gasoline and kerosene cans against the wall. His workshop would never have passed a fire inspection in the States, or in England either, for that matter, with all that naphtha, benzine, chloroform, and an assortment of what I guessed to be exotic and highly flammable fuels heaped together. Those jets use sophisticated and volatile fuels. It doesn't take much to set them off.

"It's a good thing his workshop is so far away from everyone else," I said as Fil and I made our way back toward the bridge.

"You mean the noise."

"That, plus all that stuff he's got piled against the wall. If he ever lights a match in there, you'll be missing part of your county."

It was almost dark when Fil and I reached the Hall, but I can't say I felt comfortable about going inside. No lights were on and Fil noticed my hesitation. "It'll be better when we get a fire going in the Great Room. Come along." I stayed as close to him as I could.

He was about to open the door when I grabbed his hand. "Now what the dickens is the matter?" he said.

"Don't go in, Fil," I whispered. "Someone's in there."

"How can you be so sure?" he whispered back. "The door is closed and I don't hear anything."

"I just know, believe me. There's someone in there."

"All right, then. Wait a moment, I'll get something."

He was gone for a very long time, maybe a minute and a half, and I stood rooted to the spot, feeling awful inside, knowing that there was something on the other side of the door. The hallway was pitch dark and I heard Fil coming long before I saw him. He was carrying an ancient spear which he shoved up to my face. It was one of those two-edge affairs, with one pointed end and a blade on the side. I've looked it up since and it's called a halberd. Anyway he thrust it at me.

"Here, you can use this to defend yourself." He cocked

his head outside the door and then made a sour face. "You must be out of your mind," he squeezed out in a thin voice. "Go ahead, open it."

I didn't have much choice. Very slowly I turned the knob. There was one click and then, all by itself, the great door swung inward. I peered around the room and barely made out the fading light in one of the long windows across the room. There was no point standing there.

I took three steps forward, making not the slightest sound. My inheritance of stealth and silence was in each movement.

I looked. Nothing. Another step. I looked. Nothing. Another step. Something.

Someone had a firm grip on my shoulder.

9

Seven Uncle Morgans—Gone!

The viselike grip on my shoulder wasn't familiar. The voice was.

"Eh, *chico*. Where you going with that thing?"

"What the devil? Ramón!" I cried as I sagged against him. "Hey, brother, it's good to see you!"

There he was before me. The great Ramón. My beacon of strength, my security blanket. For the first time, the Great Room seemed cozy. Ramón's presence shrunk that football field down to a warm hogan.

Fil was right. Ramón looked more like my father than the rest of us Garcías, taller and powerfully built. And anyone who tells you that Indians have cold, chiseled faces without emotion hasn't met Ramón. Because even in that poor light, I detected a hint of a crooked smile. Ramón gingerly put the halberd down and gripped my arm firmly, and that was all the warm emotion I needed.

"You remember Fil," I said, breaking away.

"Sure. Good to see you again, Fil."

"Can you stay long?" Fil asked. His offer, I could tell by

his voice, was more than good manners. Ramón's presence was comforting, even to one who hardly knew him.

Ramón's answer disappointed both of us. "I wish I could, but I must be in London early tomorrow. I'll have to drive back tonight."

My voice gave away my disappointment, and maybe a little hysteria, too. "Oh, come on, stay a little longer."

"No, I'm sorry. Can't miss my appointment. Maybe I'll come back later," he answered firmly, and I knew that was as much as we were going to get out of him.

"You will stay for dinner?" Fil asked.

"I'd like that."

At least Sudbury Hall would feel safe for a few more hours.

Dinner was a ball. It was great having my brother at the same table. Ramón may not be much of a talker, but a good listener he is. Talking much too fast, I told him about all the weirdo things that had happened since I arrived at Sudbury Hall.

It was good to see Fil come to life, too. He abandoned his reserve and heaved himself into my monologue, making corrections and additions as I unwound the tale. Ramón ate slowly, silently, acknowledging our remarks with a nod now and then.

"What do you think?" I finally asked, out of breath.

Ramón put his napkin on the table and sat back. "Okay, let's go over it. One, your real estate agent, Sage, told you about a legend of ghosts, ancestors, and death. Two, your cousin—Reggie—that his name?"

"Reggie, that's right," Fil said.

"Okay. Reggie found a diary confirming what Sage told you. And you found an old letter reconfirming it."

"Right."

"When you heard the horn for the first time, the Wing Commander's lady friend disappeared. And the second time, it was your dog, Beowolf."

Fil nodded wordlessly.

"Now. Here in the manor you've seen a ghost that led you into the same room each time, pulled at a sword, and vanished. True?"

"True."

"Okay. Now. Who are the people who have access to the manor? Parkhurst . . . Does Parkhurst have a wife living here?"

I waited for Fil's answer with interest.

"Yes," he told us, "but she keeps to herself in the servants' quarters and seldom ventures out."

"Okay. Parkhurst and his wife have ready access. You and your cousin, Reggie. How about your parents—you've notified them?"

"Yes, of course, but they're on a ship en route to Australia and won't land for another fortnight. Actually, I hated to tell them enough to alarm them. It's been so long since they've had a holiday."

"Okay, your parents are out of it. Then there's Sage, who as real estate agent knows the place well. The inventor, Matlock, who spends most of his time working on a jet engine. Inspector Wakefield, the customs inspector. Is Wakefield a big fellow with a red beard?"

"Yes, that's right," I said eagerly. "Do you know him?"

"I think I met him once in connection with a . . . matter that concerned us both." Ramón's words were guarded, but my stomach turned over. Once again my suspicions were aroused about the dangerous nature of his work. "A good man," Ramón went on. "He's working on a smuggling case now, you say?"

"That's right."

"Then he's probably just as glad to have Matlock looking after his place while he's gone. But Matlock's often away, too, testing his engine. True? Okay. Now we have a young woman who has shown interest in the Hall and was perhaps seen starting a fire in Wakefield's cutter. Who did you say saw her?"

"Ben Richmond," I told him. "And listen, Ramón, I think he's a likely suspect in this thing. He was following Fil and me or Reggie along the coast today—and he's a pure phony!" Fil stared at me. "He claims he's a mystery writer," I rushed on, "but he's not even a mystery *reader!* Anyone who reads mysteries knows that you won't find Perry Mason in any book by John Dickson Carr. The Perry Mason mysteries are written by Erle Stanley Gardner! But when I mentioned John Dickson Carr's Perry Mason to Richmond, he didn't even catch it!"

Fil's jaw had dropped, but Ramón only gave me his slow smile. "Eh, little brother, you've grown up on me. So. Our Ben Richmond has a poor cover story. That I am glad to know.

"Okay. Now. The college student was seen, or was said to have been seen by Ben Richmond-with-a-poor-cover. And she was seen by the two of you with Cousin Reggie, and Reggie had been carrying a hunting horn. Good. This leaves who?"

"Wing Commander Selkirk," I told him. "The ex-RAF man. I told you he'd estimated the value of the sword for Fil. Oh, yes, and Mr. Cravatt, the antique dealer."

Ramón nodded and, folding his arms across his chest, stared out the window.

At length I prodded him. "What do you think we should do?"

Ramón's eyes focused on me. "You should take care of yourself. You, too, Fil. But this old legend, it comes from the writings of—who was it?"

"Edmund, Sixth Earl of Sudbury."

"You will loan them to me, Fil?"

"Yes, of course," Fil said at once.

"Good. Okay. And your dog Beowolf. Beowolf?" Ramón repeated. "Yes. Have you advertised for him?"

Fil tucked his chin in. "Why, uh—actually, no. It didn't seem a likely way to find him."

"Yes, true. But if the dog is still alive, someone may have seen him. The most obvious ways often get the best results."

Fil recovered quickly. "I can do both things straight-away. I'll fetch Edmund's account of the legend, and Park-hurst will call to London for the advertisement."

Parkhurst, who had just entered and was hovering over Ramón, moved his head a touch, which meant that he would see to it. Funny thing, even ol' Parkhurst was affected by Ramón's magic, his way of dominating a room without even being aware of it. Parkhurst, who so far had contrived to ignore me completely, was bent upon serving Ramón hand and foot.

At this point, Reggie gangled in. He helped himself to food from the sideboard, sprawled in a chair, and sipped and munched away.

"Reggie, this is my brother, Ramón," I said to him.

Reggie's hair slid back and his wide eyes peeked out. He seemed genuinely surprised to find someone else in the room and grinned. "A pleasure," he said to Ramón. Then his face took on a dreamy glow, and I waited for what I knew was coming next. "I say, Mr. García, will you be here long? If you don't mind my saying so, you'd make a fantastic model. Would you—do you think—could I paint your portrait?"

While Ramón was getting himself out of that, I caught Fil giving his artist cousin long and searching looks. I wondered if he was pumping up his courage to ask him the vital question: "What were you doing at The Three Rams today, old top, and with a hunting horn yet?"

Fil finally asked, "Did you enjoy your visit in the village, Reggie?"

The handsome face came out, startled, and the mouth answered. "I wasn't—I didn't go to town today, Filbert. I've been—working right here in the Hall."

"Oh," was all Fil could reply.

Ramón took in the situation, said nothing, and I'm sure understood everything.

Fil's question hadn't put Reggie on the run, but it did speed up his spooning. He finished his meal, grinned self-consciously, and left the room.

Fil excused himself shortly after and went for the documents by his ancestor, Edmund.

Ramón and I were alone. We didn't have to say much to understand each other.

"You're frightened, Herb?"

"I hate to admit it, but yes, I'm scared to death. There's something really bad going on here."

"I know."

"You do?"

Ramón pointed one long finger toward the ceiling and it slowly circled the room. "It is in the air."

"Come on, Ramón, quit playing strong silent Redman with me. What have you figured out from all this?"

For an answer I got a crooked smile. "Enough. What you told me is interesting. And—"

"And what?"

"And in the words of the Westerns, plenty paleface here speak with forked tongues."

We both laughed.

Fil came back with the documents and showed Ramón both samples of Edmund's writing.

"This one," he explained, "tells about the legend of the hunting horn. If you check both the handwritings you'll see that they are the same."

Ramón looked and then folded one of the sheets back up. "Okay if I keep this a while? I'll return it."

"If you're Herb's brother, then you must be on the up and up. I'll trust you with it."

Ramón put the paper into his breast pocket. "Okay, kids. It's been good seeing you, but I have to get going now."

"You are fortunate," Fil said. "If you stayed around here much longer, you'd have to suffer the same fate as the rest of us. Arthur Matlock's jet engine, Phoebe. The noise is quite shattering."

Ramón was interested. "Yes, I'm sorry to miss that. I have a fondness for machines. Maybe I'll stop by his place and take a look."

"Ramón studied physics in college," I explained. "He even built his own little car once."

"I may say a quick hello to Inspector Wakefield," Ramón added, more outgoing than usual. "He is a good man."

Ramón now seemed in a hurry to get to wherever he was headed. We went with him out the front door. "I suppose you have a car around here somewhere, unless you walked down from London." With Ramón even that was possible.

"No," he answered. "I was in a hurry so I drove. My car is in back."

And it was, but I would have spent a half hour looking

for it. It was a neat little sports car and secretive Ramón had it hidden off the road under some trees.

"Ramón, you're tremendous. And I still don't know what you do for a living, but whatever it is, it sure is obvious that no one else is going to find out either."

He shook my hand warmly as he slid behind the wheel. "Good luck. Be careful. And look after your friend."

"And who's going to look after me?"

He just grinned.

When the little car jetted away, a lot of me went with it. The warmth and security were gone. I was back at cold, creepy Sudbury Hall, and I didn't like it.

It was dark now and the lights from inside seemed perhaps a shade more reassuring than the blackness that shrouded the grounds of the manor. We walked around to the front. The door was still standing open where we had left it when we went out with Ramón.

"I must admit," Fil said, sprinting for the door, "it is creepy out here."

I was right beside him and then my ignorant feet stopped because my stupid head registered something that wasn't right.

"Fil, look at Uncle Morgan."

He followed my finger to the pedestal in front of the house that held the bust of the founder of the firm.

"I don't believe it . . . I don't believe it . . . I don't believe it," he muttered.

What he didn't believe was the simple fact that the pedestal was empty. The bust of Uncle Morgan was gone.

He raced over to the stone stand. "Where could it have gone? This is preposterous!"

"Oh, I don't know, Fil ol' buddy. It's not any crazier

than anything else that has been going on here. Could it have fallen off?"

"That's even more preposterous!" he snapped. But I noticed he looked over the ground just to make sure.

I took him by the arm and led him to the manor. "We'll freeze to death out here, Fil. Come inside and we'll worry about Uncle Morgan's head later."

He was completely dazed when we entered the Hall. I was just as dazed after I took three steps inside. "Now take it easy, Filbert," I said soothingly.

"I am quite all right," he assured me, taking in a chestful of air and pulling himself up tall.

"You may not be when I'm finished," I said. He didn't speak. "You know that other bust of Morgan that stands beside the door of the Great Room?"

"Why yes, of course."

"Well, it doesn't."

He looked and I got hit with another, "Good Lord!"

That bust was gone too.

We made our way into the Great Room, sat down, and just breathed as slowly and as carefully as we could. If I could have found the strength, I would have run anywhere, as far away from Sudbury Hall as possible. Maybe it'll help if I scream, I thought. I gave the idea a good deal of consideration and decided that breathing would do for the minute. The way things were going I might not have too much of that left to do.

"We can't just sit here," Fil suddenly burst out. "Let's take a look around."

So we started tromping through Sudbury Hall, and every place where there had been a bust of Uncle Morgan, there wasn't. We counted. "That makes number seven, Herb. Seven Uncle Morgans gone."

"That's all that were down here," Fil said. He was calmer. One missing bust had rattled him. Now there was a pattern. Someone or something was picking up all the busts of the great man. Things had moved from the realm of the supernatural to the real and the tangible. Who was doing this? And the bigger question—Why?

10

Gentlemen, Please!

We climbed a winding staircase to the second floor. Sudbury Hall now seemed more forbidding than when I had first set eyes on it. I stepped cautiously, looked cautiously, and breathed cautiously. I sensed that Fil was just as oppressed by the strange mood that had fallen over the house as I was.

"How many more are up here?" I asked in a whisper.

"I don't recall exactly." Fil waxed philosophical. "It is odd the way a person can walk past something every day and not really notice. I feel rather dense not being able to tell you."

We were proceeding down a very long corridor with perhaps twenty doors on our left. Fil stared at each one as we passed and then stopped at one in particular.

"Anything wrong?" I asked.

"Not at all. It's just that this one is a box room, or as you say in the States, a storeroom. I know there are a great many paintings in there, but I can't recall if there are any busts of Morgan."

"Let's look."

The room was dark, even in comparison to the dimly lit hallway which had occasional electric lights spaced too far apart. But there wasn't any light here. And I was surprised to discover that there wasn't a light switch either.

"No electricity, Fil?"

"Not in every part of the manor. Good Lord, man, it would have cost a packet to wire this entire place. Stand fast, there should be some candles about."

Fill rummaged around for a few minutes and then I heard a match strike and three candles on a thin iron candelabrum came to life. Weird shadows danced over the ancient walls, walls that were completely covered with paintings of the past.

"Hold the candles up a little, Fil. Let's have a better look."

Like everything else in Sudbury Hall, the box room was enormous and practically empty, except for some boxes here and there and a great many canvases on the walls, and stacked against the walls.

"No busts of Morgan, Herb. Shall we move on?"

"Momentito. One little moment. Let me have a look at some of these paintings. Do you know who all these kinfolk are?"

Fil shook his head. "Not really. It has taken me some time just to learn the important ones, the masters of the manor. Many of these are wives and cousins and nieces and nephews, some going back centuries."

"How about those canvases stacked against the wall?"

"I imagine they are more of the same. You must remember in those days they didn't have photography. So instead of merely taking a snapshot as we do today, anybody who was anybody at all had his portrait painted."

"It also helped fill up some pretty big, empty walls," I

pointed out. I started to look over the dusty paintings that were propped against the wall. Fil was right, more of the same. Men with plumed hats and silk knickers and ladies in elegant gowns. And then I came to one that was different. Very different. I pulled it out and held it up for Fil to see. He brought his candles closer.

"That is definitely *not* one of the family."

"I didn't think so."

What I was holding was a large canvas showing a huge, handsome man in the middle of a swagger, if there is such a thing. He stood before a mountain of chests from which jewels and gold ornaments were bulging and hanging out. One hand was on his hip and the other held a sword. Behind him stood a group of men as ugly as any you've ever seen, like something out of a pirate movie. The man was considerably larger than anyone else in the picture, and it wasn't just the artist's perspective in drawing the scene. Our swaggering man was tall, husky, and dressed all in black.

You guessed it. So did I. Black Dan.

"I never realized we had a picture of that scoundrel," Fil commented. "I must admit, if not for the malicious grin on his face, he was quite an imposing figure."

The more I stared at this bad guy from out of the past, the more familiar he became. "You know, Fil, he looks like someone I know."

"From home?"

"Maybe, but I don't think so. Seems like somebody I've met recently."

"Perhaps on the boat, Herb. Americans say we English do tend to have similar features."

"I guess that's it. But I sure wish I could remember."

"No point hanging about here any longer. I'm still concerned about those missing busts of Morgan."

We left the room and continued down the long corridor. We passed a point where another hallway cut into the one we were traveling.

"Do you have any particular place in mind?" I asked, after taking a quick glance down the other hallway.

"If my memory serves me, I do believe there's supposed to be another bust of Morgan down at the end of this hallway."

"Don't let me ruin your day for you, Fil, but there's also a Morgan in the hallway we just passed!

"Exactly what do you mean?" Fil asked in a low voice.

"I think I saw Morgan himself—not his statue—hiding in one of the doorways."

"The same one we saw before?"

"If you mean the ghost, yes."

"What do you suggest we do?"

"He's probably waiting for the sound of our footsteps to die out. So let's let 'em and when we get to the end of the hallway we'll wait in a doorway ourselves and see if he comes our way. Two can play the old waiting-in-the-doorway game. Okay?"

Fil led the way. "The shadow of death," I heard him mutter once. We reached the end of the corridor and then on tiptoe doubled back some twenty feet to squeeze ourselves into a doorway. We waited.

But not for long. The ghost of Morgan, Fourth Earl of Sudbury, came at great speed into our corridor, turned, and headed away from us as if there were someplace he had to get to and fast.

I guess he thought he had outsmarted us, but a second later he knew better. Fil took off after him like a shot, with me not too far behind. Ghost or no ghost, Morgan knew we were after him. He picked up speed, holding one glowing, gloved hand to his glowing, plumed hat so he wouldn't lose it as he highballed down the corridor. He turned a corner and a few seconds later Fil made the same screeching turn.

When I made that turn myself I came upon Fil standing in another dimly lit corridor, scratching his head.

"The old boy's gone?"

"Afraid so, Herb. He just vanished."

"Do you still think that was ectoplasm you were chasing?"

"I surrender. That was no ghost. I could hear him breathing hard as he tried to outdistance me. He must have gone behind these walls." Fil searched the long expanse of paneled walls. "But where?"

"We could look all night and not find him. Let's go back downstairs and think this thing out," I suggested.

The fire in the Great Room was reassuring. I was beginning to look upon that oversized living room as a refuge. I knew what was supposed to be in it and could sense at once if things weren't right. At least I had the feeling I could.

Fil was thoughtful for a while and I didn't disturb his thinking. Sure, this was strange as could be as far as I was concerned, but I was just a visitor. This was *his* house. All these weird things that were happening affected *him*. There was a big difference. What was a problem and a mental exercise for me, was real, perhaps life and death, for him.

He looked up at me. "Let us see if we can reason this out," he said calmly. "First, the ghost of Morgan, Fourth Earl of Sudbury, is definitely not a ghost."

"Correct. Or at least the one we just chased isn't."

"Aha, then you do believe in ghosts."

"I'm not saying yes and I'm not saying no," I answered, looking around me. If there was a real ghost of Morgan,

Fourth Earl of Sudbury, lurking about those premises, I didn't see any point in getting him mad. "But the one we've seen is a phony."

"The next question," Fil said holding up one finger for emphasis, "is why?"

"Why do *you* think, Filbert ol' buddy?"

"I haven't the foggiest idea."

"May I make a guess?"

"Be my guest."

I started pacing. I do my best thinking when I'm roving. "How about this, Fil. Question: why would anyone dress up in a glowing Morgan, Fourth Earl of Sudbury, costume? Answer: to get you to notice him. He is hard *not* to notice in that phosphorescent costume."

"Is that what you think it is?"

"It's some kind of luminous paint, wouldn't you say? And why would a ghost be so conspicuous? Because he wants us to notice him. And why does he want us to notice him?"

"So we won't notice something else," Fil answered with a triumphant ring to his voice.

"Sounds logical to me, Filbert. Now the next question is, what doesn't he want us to notice?"

Triumph turned to defeat. "I haven't the foggiest," Fil muttered.

"Let's try this for size. The ghost, or whoever is playing the ghost, doesn't want us to notice that something else is going on in this house."

"Of course, and that's why he's been so obvious about that sword!" Fil pointed over the fireplace. "You know, each time I've chased him in here he's had plenty of time to get it! It isn't hard to get off the wall. So, he really didn't want it after all. He just wanted us to *think* that he wanted it—to draw our attention away from something else in this house. And that brings us back to the same question. What is happening in this house?"

"Do you remember that line written by your esteemed ancestor Morgan, Fourth Earl of Sudbury, about Black Dan?"

"I don't follow you, Herb."

"I can't forget it. It's been bothering me since I first walked into this place. You mentioned that Morgan had written something like . . . 'Black Dan, that scoundrel, has been storing his contraband in my Small Room!' That may not be the exact way he wrote it, but it gives you the general idea."

"Right-o," Fil said. "Now I remember. But how does that help explain what else is going on in this house that I'm not supposed to know?"

"Like this: where is there a *small room* in this place outside the servants' quarters?"

Fil stood up and smashed his fist into his palm. "Of course! How stupid of me!"

"Then am I correct in assuming that there really are no *small* rooms in the manor?"

"You knew the answer to that one before you asked, you sly dog. So the Small Room my ancestor mentioned must be somewhere else. Most likely a hidden room, maybe—"

"Under this house," I cut in. "I feel sure it's under the east wing, and that's what this nonsense with glowing ghosts, horns that bleat in the night, and that sword is all about. All are designed to get your attention away from that Small Room, where someone is playing the same game that was played hundreds of years ago—smuggling."

"Smuggling!" Fil repeated as if in a trance. "I find that hard to believe."

"What else can it be?"

I waited a long time for his answer. "I don't know," he finally answered. "But smuggling, I mean that is going a bit far. If it is smuggling, then who and how?"

"I can't answer those questions just now, Fil, but since I arrived I've had the strange feeling that everyone I've met isn't exactly what he or she is supposed to be."

I had gone too fast for him. "No, no, Herb," he complained. "I'll go along with you that the figure we saw of Morgan, Fourth Earl of Sudbury, was no ghost. But the rest—I mean this business about smuggling and my friends and neighbors being involved—that is simply too much for me to accept."

"I'm not accusing anyone, Filbert. I'm just bringing up the fact that some strange things have been happening. The next question is *who* and *how,* as you put it. If it is smuggling, then it's being done very cleverly, for Inspector Wakefield is certainly no fool."

"There is one point that makes me think you may be on to something, Herb, and that's the business about the Small Room. If my ancestor wrote that there was a Small Room in this manor, then there must be one someplace. And as you suggest, I suppose it could be under the house, and at the opposite end. But if that's the case, how does one get to it?"

"There's probably an entrance to it right here in the house. And outside, too, if my guess is correct. I'd say from the river that winds behind the house."

"Wait a minute. . . . Okay, I've got it. Someone could bring a boat from the English Channel down the little river and then—"

"And then, Filbert, somewhere, hidden in the underbrush along the banks, there's a passageway from that river into this house, to a room somewhere below us. Are you game to have a look?"

"It's probably the best way to find out. Let's give it a try, and we had better wear something warm."

"Also bring a flashlight."

"Flashlight? Oh—over here it's called a torch."

"Call it a hockey puck if you like, Fil ol' buddy, only bring something so we can see where we're going."

He laughed as we left the Great Room.

At first I didn't think there was a moon, because it was absolutely pitch black as we stepped out into the night. Then the clouds parted, big black puffy clouds, and there was a very round yellow moon. When it was out we didn't need the flashlight.

We scooted across the lawn and into the trees. Then it got very dark and as we drew closer to the place where ground ended and air began, I stepped more cautiously. I didn't want to take the first big step to the hospital. Fil kept the light on so we could see where we were going.

Grandfather would have been proud of me that night. I looked and sniffed at the air like an animal trying to pick up the scent of game. And found it.

I wasn't sure what or who it was at first, but again, a strong feeling churned inside me that Fil and I were not alone in the woods. I said nothing as I trudged behind my English friend. Better make sure before I open my big mouth.

We were almost to the cliff when just beyond the beam of Fil's light my eye caught a swift movement.

Aha, someone was moving behind us, flitting from tree to tree. I slowed down.

"Behind us. There's someone back there. Let's not waste any time." With that, I spun and charged at the tree. Sure enough there was someone there, because as I punched out with my best tomahawk-throwing arm, a hand caught me and flung me to the ground as if I were a tennis ball being thumped off a racket. As I went down, I saw Fil have a go at the large figure. He bounced, too, and the flashlight went flying. We both charged again and were caught by two strong hands.

"Gentlemen, please!"

The voice was familiar. Just then a cloud parted and we both stared stupidly at the annoyed, but still pretty face of Agatha Howe.

11

What About Reggie?

There comes a time when even English reserve goes to pieces. This was it. Fil exploded.

"Good Lord, Miss Howe, what's the meaning of this!"

The girl, tall and erect and looking even more menacing in her black coat, stammered. "I–I–didn't mean any harm. . . . You b–b–both came at me so suddenly."

"Never mind that, now," Fil fired back, getting to his feet and meeting her eye to eye. "What are you doing here?"

"Why, as you know, I'm doing a research paper."

"Baloney," I put in, cutting her short.

"Excuse me?" she asked weakly.

"That's American for 'stuff and nonsense!' Miss Howe. How about telling us the truth? You've beat that *I'm doing a research paper* business to death. You may be a student all right, but you're also someone else. And I think I know who."

Both Fil and the girl turned their startled faces on me. "Filbert, step back a few paces and take a good look at our Agatha!"

He did, waiting a moment for the dark clouds to part and

the moon to illuminate the girl's face and figure. Agatha Howe stood silently, wondering what we were up to. I think she knew.

Fil stared and then murmured, "She looks like Black Dan!"

"That's what crossed my mind," I added. "When I saw that painting of Dan in your box room, I said he looked familiar. Now I know why."

The girl's erect figure sagged and she sighed, "Oh, all right, if you must be difficult about it. I am a descendant of Black Dan." She glanced pleadingly from my face to Fil's, "But I assure you, I meant no harm to anyone."

"Exactly what do you want?" Fil asked.

The girl relaxed, and became more for real as she put aside her pretense and for the first time spoke the truth, rather charmingly and in earnest. I think she felt better about it. "My story isn't all fiction, you see. I am a university student and I am doing a paper on the history of the county. Inasmuch as Black Dan is my ancestor, not a very illustrious one I admit, but still a blood relation, I naturally became interested in knowing more about it. I started out simply to find out as much as I could. I didn't want anyone to know I was related to Dan, because I thought that would focus attention on me and I wouldn't learn what I wanted to know."

That part was okay. If she had announced that she was related to Dan, feelings in the area might have very well turned against her. Black Dan wasn't even a welcome memory in that part of the world.

"But why all the snooping?" Fil asked.

"I am sorry about that, Mr. Golightly," she answered, sounding genuinely apologetic. "You see, it didn't take me long to realize that something was very much amiss at Sudbury Hall."

"Like what?" I asked.

"Well, all that talk about the ghost of Morgan, and the horn sounding. I have researched the history of the manor quite carefully. The legend about Morgan's ghost coming back to avenge his murder appears nowhere. The legend is of fairly recent origin."

"It appears in the letters I showed you," Fil answered.

"Yes, and that still perplexes me."

"Anything else?" I asked.

"Well, this smuggling business caught my attention at once. I have heard that Inspector Wakefield is quite concerned about a large amount of contraband reaching the coast near here. Because of Black Dan my interest was heightened. As you know, he used this manor to warehouse his smuggled goods and the thought struck me that perhaps someone was using the same technique."

"That thought struck us too," I admitted. "Have you learned anything more?"

The girl shook her head. "I haven't. And that's why I've been staying so close to the manor."

Fil had cooled down. "I don't know if what you are telling us is true or not, Miss Howe. But I do know you aren't making things any easier for us."

"It is the truth, Mr. Golightly. I swear that it is the truth."

Fil ignored her remark. "Please, do us a favor, Miss Howe."

"Anything."

"Go back to The Three Rams and leave Sudbury Hall alone. If we learn anything we'll tell you, I promise."

The girl looked and sounded despondent. "I have made

a proper mess of things, haven't I! Please forgive me, I meant no harm. I shall do as you say. And again, I am indeed sorry." She started away and once more I was struck by how closely her large frame and face resembled her ignominious ancestor. (I thought I'd throw in a big word! Why should Filbert have all the fun?)

"One more thing, Miss Howe," I called. She turned.

"Why did you set fire to the *Dorset*?"

"I had nothing to do with that," she shouted, and I was glad she wasn't within hitting distance.

She vanished into the darkness.

"What do you make of *that,* Herb?" Fil said after he was sure she was out of earshot.

"I think she's telling the truth."

"If she didn't set fire to the *Dorset,* who did? You remember Ben Richmond said he saw her. Do you think he was lying?"

"Could be," I answered, "but I've got another idea about that fire and about quite a few other things that have been happening here. Just about anybody and everybody could be telling a little fib here and there."

"Even Inspector Wakefield?" Fil asked, as if the possibility really was unthinkable.

"Even Parkhurst as far as I'm concerned, Filbert ol' buddy. At this point I don't believe nobody and nuthin'. Let's find out for ourselves. Where's the flashlight?"

"Sorry, but it's gone. It went flying when Miss Howe hurled me to the ground. Good Lord, but she's strong!"

"It must run in her family. Come on, maybe a visit to the river will produce some answers."

We edged our way very slowly toward the cliff and then down the trail that led to the small river below. When the moon broke through the clouds, everything was fine. And when it didn't, we stopped dead in our tracks and waited for the light. It took a while but we finally made our way to the rock-strewn beach. The sound of water moving steadily along enveloped us.

"It seems quiet enough," Fil commented.

"But for how long, Filbert?"

"What did you expect to find?"

"As I said earlier, if smuggling is the game, and if there is a Small Room under your manor, then this is a likely way to it. And after our run in with Morgan, Fourth Earl of Sudbury, tonight, I got the feeling that someone will be using this li'l ol' river tonight."

"Really, Herb, you have far too many feelings. I am not saying your idea is completely wrong, but it may be a bit far-fetched." Then he started arguing with himself. "But then again, Miss Howe had the same line of thought, you know, smuggling. But she could be on the wrong track also. We mustn't let our imagination run away with good clear thinking. After all—"

He didn't finish his monologue, because just about then we both heard the same thing, the sound of a motor. We dove for the cover of some bushes along the bank of the stream and peered out, waiting and hoping that the nasty black clouds would let the moon peek through.

I said we heard a motor and I don't want to give you the impression it was a high-powered speedboat or anything like that. It was more of a muffled put-put. But it was a steady put-put and coming toward us from a mass of underbrush just ahead of us.

The clouds were working for us that night, because just as those bushes parted, the moon came out for an instant and we saw what our senses told us we should not be seeing —a small motorboat coming right out of the bushes!

"Incredible!" Fil exclaimed in a pitched whisper.

"Kind of makes you think you're losing your marbles, doesn't it? Weirdest thing I've ever seen."

"There must be a channel under those bushes that goes to the house under the ground."

"What else could it be?"

"Shushhhh."

We hardly breathed as we waited. The put-putting came close, closer, still closer, along the opposite bank of the river. The clouds came back but we did get a good enough peep to see that someone was sitting in the boat steering a course down the river toward the English Channel.

I held my breath and peered and strained my eyes. No luck. "Did you see who it was, Fil?"

"Blast! It was too dark and he or she was huddled in the back. It could have been anyone."

The put-putting was dying away, and Fil began leading us back toward the trail that led to the manor house.

"I see it now," Fil told me. "We were supposed to be rushing pell-mell after Uncle Morgan's ghost toward the other side of the manor, while the smugglers started the motor and left the Small Room."

I stopped him. "Fil, do you think we can follow this little beach all the way down to where the river empties into the channel?"

"I don't know. Let's give it a try. Perhaps we can find out who was in the boat."

We trudged along the banks. In places we were slowed by the sudden rise of land that moved right to the water making a small cliff. It wasn't easy in the dark to do much climbing safely. But we kept on, pushed by curiosity and even anger. I know we both had reached our boiling points.

It stayed dark for a long time and in the distance we

would occasionally hear that put-put of the small boat. Just as we would gain on it, we'd have to climb over some hill or fight our way through some bushes, picking unruly branches out of our faces. We kept following the river.

It got wider. A good sign. "We must be getting near the channel."

"Look up ahead, Herb. There's the road and that little humpbacked bridge. We were there before."

We climbed the embankment and from the stone bridge got our best look that night of the little boat moving out into the vast English Channel. Only the situation had changed.

"Do you see two figures in that boat now, Herb?"

"It looks that way. Someone else has gotten in. Do you think one of them is Matlock? I mean, this little river goes right by his place."

"Could be, Herb. Sounds right. But I wonder who the other one is?"

"Before we're sure it's Matlock, let's have a look at his place."

"It has to be Matlock. Don't you see, Herb! It makes sense! The boat went right by his place. He certainly would have heard it, if nothing else. And if he heard it he'd be out on the banks looking to see who and what it was."

"Let's be positive."

"We're wasting time, but all right."

We hurried the short distance to Matlock's work building. The light was on but the door was locked. It was very quiet.

"See, Herb, I just knew it was him."

I peeked in the closed window. Arthur Matlock was bending over his jet engine. Fil saw my face and looked in for himself.

"I keep coming up with wrong answers," he complained. "But Herb, don't you think he would have heard the boat go by?"

"Maybe not. His place is closed up pretty tight and if he was preoccupied with Phoebe, he might not have heard it at all. I mean, here we are right outside his place and he doesn't seem to know we're here."

"Another good theory shot to pieces. I think we had better get back to the house. That other mystery still has me depressed."

"What other mystery?"

"The busts of Morgan, Fourth Earl of Sudbury. Where have they gone?"

"That's a mystery all right. Let's get back."

I was glad, even thrilled that we left Matlock's place when we did. When we got halfway down the road to the manor, I suddenly knew why his door and window were closed . . . Phoebe. She came to life with a roar you wouldn't believe. I thought my eardrums were going to burst! And even when we flew through the front doors of Sudbury Hall they were still painful.

"No wonder everyone's complaining!" I said when we had shut the heavy doors behind us and muffled Phoebe's roar a little. "It's inhuman."

"I'm afraid it will go on like that for over an hour. Actually, it's not ear-splitting here in the manor. You'll grow accustomed to it."

Fil started up the wide circular staircase to the second floor. "I should like to know what's happened to those busts of Morgan."

I followed him warily. Our last trip around the house had made me a bit shaky! I wasn't used to ghosts coming out of the walls and zooming away to disappear into other walls. So I looked real carefully as we made our way through the house. "Do you know where there are other busts of your noble ancestor?"

"There should be one down the end of this corridor," Fil answered, trying to peer ahead down the hallway in what was very poor light. When we reached the end of our journey we found an empty pedestal.

Fil looked pained. "It simply doesn't make sense! What could have possibly happened to them?"

"I can answer that, Fil. Someone took them."

"But why!"

"I don't know. Let's look a little more."

He led the way up another flight of stairs to the third floor, gloomier and even darker than the second floor. "I think there are a few more busts of Morgan up here."

"What else is up here?" I asked, staying close to Fil and wishing I had eyes in the back of my skull. I didn't like being so far from the Great Room. It's funny the way you get accustomed to things. At first the Great Room had terrified me, but now it was friendly territory, perhaps the only friendly territory in the manor. The farther we moved from it the more my stomach protested and my nerves danced up and down my uncomfortable body.

"There is very little here but empty rooms," Fil answered leading the way. "Except for Reggie's studio."

"Where's that?"

"Just ahead. Perhaps he'll have some ideas about what's happened to Morgan's busts. Although the way he's been acting lately—"

Fil didn't finish. I guess he didn't want to say the words that had to condemn his cousin and friend. Reggie had lied to him about being in town. I know that lie hurt Fil more than Reggie could realize.

"Do you think he's there?"

"Most likely, Herb. He spends most of his time up here working on his sculpture and occasional paintings."

We opened the door to Reggie's studio and found the answer to the missing busts of Morgan, Fourth Earl of Sudbury.

"Good grief!" was all Fil could squeeze out.

The room was well lighted. It was a studio with one wall of sloping glass to let in the sun. Tables were everywhere. Tables that held sculpture . . . the same sculpture. The missing busts of Morgan. But they had changed.

I gaped with my jaw hanging open like an idiot while my mind tried to comprehend what my eyes were seeing. "Why, he's bronzed them, every darn one of them!"

Fil looked from the statues to me. "Do you think he has . . . he has gone off his head?" It was tough for Fil to get that out.

"No, I don't think so. At dinner he did say that they'd look better bronzed. Who knows how an artist's mind works? And besides, he was right. They do look better bronzed!" I glanced back at the busts. "But I can't figure out why he bronzed them first and then smashed them."

"Smashed them! You're putting me on! Where?"

"On that table, Fil. There must be five of them that have been smashed with a sledge hammer or something else pretty heavy and blunt."

We moved to the table and studied the fragments of what had once been busts of Morgan, Fourth Earl of Sudbury.

"This is getting more odd by the moment," Fil cried, a desperate note in his voice. "Reggie must indeed have lost control of himself! Poor Reggie, what a strange and terrible thing to do! We must get psychiatric help for him."

Fil went on worrying out loud about Reggie's mental

condition. I slowly made my way around the room. Busts of Morgan were everywhere, and perhaps a third of them had been smashed, not with any pattern or plan, but with a randomness that smacked of desperation—as if someone had suddenly gone mad and went about bashing a statue here and a statue there.

Fil was right. It made no sense at all. Just to look at that scene made the word *madness* fly into your mind. I looked some more and the picture changed.

"Reggie didn't do this," I told Fil softly.

He stopped muttering and came back to reality, looking around until he found me. "Did you just say you didn't think Reggie smashed the busts of Morgan?"

"Brace yourself, Fil. I just stepped over him. He's sprawled out here on the floor."

12

Drugged!

I knew it! I knew the day wouldn't pass without it! The horn blew, the ghost appeared, and now— Herb—is he—?"

While Fil dashed toward me, I bent down over the prostrate form of our gentle artist. He was breathing, but not very energetically. His head rested on a pillow and a blanket covered him, which even to my not so sharp mind meant that we weren't the first to find him.

"I think he's all right, Fil, but I'm no doctor. It looks like someone else got here before we did."

"I made him comfortable," a voice intoned from behind us.

We both leaped as if we had been struck in the back of the neck by a hot poker. It wasn't what the voice said that sent sparks down our spines, it was the voice itself— Parkhurst's.

"When did you find him?" Fil asked.

"Just a few minutes ago, sir. I came by the studio and it appeared so quiet that I thought it advisable to look in. Mister Reggie is usually quite active when he is working."

By active, I gathered, he meant noisy. "Was he like this when you found him?" I asked.

"In that exact spot. I thought it best not to move him so I put the pillow under his head and covered him with a blanket in case he was in shock. I then took the liberty of leaving him to ring for the doctor."

"Good show, Parkhurst," Fil said appreciatively. "I suppose all we can do now is wait."

When the doctor arrived he shooed us into the hall, where we paced like men on trial waiting for the jury to bring in the verdict. Fil was in torment. Despite Reggie's deception, Fil liked, or more accurately, loved his cousin. Those strong feelings were hard to hide, particularly now when the artist might well be fighting for his life.

The doctor came out of the studio looking relieved. "A nasty blow on the head, but he will be fine. He's conscious and you can talk to him, chaps, but please, make your visit a short one."

Reggie was propped up in his bed in one corner of the studio. Fil raced to him and warmly gripped his shoulder. "It's marvelous to see you with your eyes open again, you old reprobate."

Reggie felt at the bandage on his head. "Someone has taken liberties with my skull."

"We can see that, Reggie," I said. "And I'm as relieved as Fil to see that you're okay. Do you remember what happened?"

"I don't remember much, Herb." Reggie shook his head slowly and yelped, "Ow, my head!" He felt the bandage. "I was bronzing the busts of Morgan for you—I say, do you like them?"

"They look much better bronzed, Reggie, as you told us they would."

Reggie leaned forward as if to clear his mind, his long black hair gone, shaved off by the doctor. It was a different Reggie. The wall that had protected him from the world had been breached. Poor guy, he looked naked.

"Did you collect all of the busts yourself, Reggie?" Fil asked gently.

"Yes, I don't think I missed any. Do you really like them bronzed?" He looked over at the table anxiously, but winced as his eyes fell upon the smashed busts. "What a wretched thing to do!" he burst out, fighting back tears. His eyes reddened, but he continued. "I needed some more newspapers to spread on my work table, so I went downstairs to get them. When I came back, I saw—Filbert, it was our ancestor, Morgan—dashing madly about, smashing all his busts!" His chest heaved with indignation.

"Take it easy, Reggie," I admonished. He fell back and I waited until he was calmer before I asked, "Do you remember what happened after that? Don't talk if it's painful."

"I went after him, of course! Ghost or no ghost, it was a shocking thing to do!"

"Good for you!" Fil cried.

Reggie worked up a weak grin. "He hit me on the head then, and that's all I remember. Fil? I'm ever so sorry about the busts."

"Not to worry, Reggie. There are still plenty of them left. There were too many of them, anyway. You get a good night's rest, and we'll talk about it more later."

A relieved expression crossed Reggie's handsome face. "At least he didn't ruin the painting."

"Which painting?" Fil asked, puzzled.

"In the corner, over there. An oil of Morgan and Black Dan. I was doing it for your family, Fil."

We both moved across the room to a draped easel. Fil

drew the covering cloth aside. A dramatic picture stood there, a picture of Morgan, Fourth Earl of Sudbury, dueling with Black Dan. In the background, a hazy, ghostly figure was blowing a hunting horn.

Suddenly one piece of the mystery made sense. I turned to Reggie. "Is that why you went into town today?"

Reggie blushed furiously. "I couldn't get the horn in proper perspective, so I went into town to buy a model. I didn't know what to say when you asked me about it, I—I wanted to surprise you, but that beastly ghost ruined it!"

"And you've been using Agatha Howe as your model for Black Dan!" Fil exclaimed triumphantly.

"That's right. You know, there's a painting of Black Dan in the box room and it looks so much like her, I asked her to sit for me while I made a few sketches. She's not really a bad sort, you know. She didn't mind at all, especially after I told her the picture was a surprise for you."

So Reggie had made the same connection we had. Although he hadn't put it into words, his artist's eyes had seen the resemblance between the villain from the past and the Amazon of a college student, Agatha Howe.

We left Reggie resting, with Parkhurst keeping watch, and went to Fil's room to get some rest ourselves. It had been a tough day and despite the weariness in my bones, I was feeling good, perhaps better than I had felt since I first set foot in Sudbury Hall. We were starting to get answers. And as I headed for dreamland, far away in the dark night I could hear Arthur Matlock's Phoebe still shrieking as if she were heralding the end of the world.

It rained hard the next day, I thought perhaps to punish us for the bit of good weather we had enjoyed. I wanted to go out and check the river and find the tunnel that I was sure led under the manor, but the downpour made me hesitate. We tried to get Inspector Wakefield on the phone, but no one answered. So Fil and I just moped around the Great Room trying to make sense of the many confusing things that had been happening at Sudbury Hall.

The first bright spot in a very tense day came in mid-afternoon when Parkhurst floated into the room and announced that there was a gentleman calling from Hampshire about the advertisement in the *Times* about Beowolf, the dog.

When Fil came back into the Great Room after his telephone conversation he was one big smile. "Beowolf's been found!" he shouted. Although I had never met the beast in person, I had heard him howl, and I was thrilled, both for Beowolf and for Fil.

"Where is he?"

"A fellow in Petersfield, in Hampshire, found him beside the road. At first he thought he was dead, but then he realized the dog had been drugged. The veterinarian has been taking care of him and just as soon as he is thoroughly cleared, Beowolf will come home. Really Herb, that's fantastic news!" Then Fil got thoughtful. "But how did your brother Ramón know that the advertisement in the *Times* would do the trick?"

"I don't think he *did* know. Ramón has a way of 'feeling' things. Maybe it's extra-sensory perception. Plus experience and common sense. Understand?"

"I'm beginning to, even if I don't really understand how."

"Let's leave it at that. Besides, Ramón is a bit weird, even if he is my brother. He just knows things. He's always been able to put two and two together and come up with eight."

Despite the gloom of the gray sky and the rain, Sudbury

Hall smiled just a little at the news of Beowolf's discovery. Even I felt better.

The high spot in the day came after dinner when Parkhurst wafted to the dinner table and announced that there was a phone call for the young Mr. García from the elder Mr. García. Which was his way of saying it was Ramón.

As I told you before, Ramón is many things, but a big talker he isn't. And when he spoke on the phone he acted as if each word was costing ten dollars. So while we didn't have a very costly conversation, I did learn two things that changed the situation at Sudbury Hall.

The first thing I learned sent me leaping back to the dining room to tell Fil. "Ramón says that letter you gave him from Edmund, the Sixth Earl of Sudbury, is a phony."

"Not really?"

"Really. He checked at a museum."

"Anything else?"

"Yes."

"Well, don't just answer like the stoic Redman of the great Western Plains. What?"

"Follow me."

"Where?"

"To Reggie's studio. I think I know why Uncle Morgan was smashing those busts of himself."

That did it. Filbert flew out of his chair and we zoomed to Reggie's studio. When we burst in we startled Reggie, who, although still bandaged, was working on what had been designed as his gift to Fil, the portrait of Uncle Morgan battling Black Dan.

His face was no longer hidden behind his hair. Now I could read his expression. It was lonely, and rather frightened. "Reggie," I said, "I want you to think real hard. Do you know which of these busts is the one that stood on the pedestal in front of the house?"

Reggie, still holding his palette, advanced to one of the work tables and thoughtfully put the end of his paintbrush in his mouth. "Let me see." He hesitated and then pointed with his brush. "That one, I think."

"Are you sure, Reggie?" I pleaded.

He made an unhappy face. "Can't be positive. It's that one or the one beside it."

"Fil, do you have any objections if I bash it?"

"If it will help clear up this shroud of mystery, go right ahead. What's one more or less?"

I bashed and found a lot of pieces of bronzed plaster. Both men stared at me.

"Well, Herb?"

"Nothing. Let me try the one beside it."

Whammo went the hammer, and pieces flew everywhere. And I found what I hoped I would find. A piece of paper. Reggie put his hand over the shattered bust of Morgan.

"Why, there was a compartment in the base!" he exclaimed.

"Is that what Morgan was after when he came in here and smashed those other busts, Herb?" asked Fil.

"Ramón suggested it might be something like that. Let's have a look." I unrolled the paper. It was a crudely drawn map of the coast, showing the dock where the *Dorset* was normally berthed and a dotted line that obviously was the direction she had been or would be traveling. I showed it to Fil.

"It is making sense now, Herb. A good deal of sense." He pointed his finger at the drawing of the boat and the dotted line marking her course. "Someone was trying to tell someone else where the *Dorset* would be going last night. Is that what you make of it?"

"You're batting a thousand."

"Batting a thousand?" Reggie blinked.

"That's a baseball term. It means a perfect score," Fil explained.

"I think your bust of Morgan in front of the house was what spies call a drop, a place to leave messages. When one party found out where the *Dorset* would be going, he would make this map and then leave it for the other party to find."

"What is this one party and another party nonsense?" Reggie demanded.

"Smuggling," Fil answered.

"How vulgar!" Reggie exclaimed and went back to his painting.

Fil and I were completing our own picture.

"But how could anyone know where the *Dorset* would be going last night, Herb? Didn't Inspector Wakefield tell us that he didn't know himself until perhaps half an hour before he put to sea? If one of the crew was in on this, he would certainly notice the man's absence directly after they had planned their course."

"The man wasn't in the crew, Fil."

"Who, then?"

"Think. Filbert ol' buddy. Who else might possibly be around when the inspector and his men planned their trip for the night?"

"Of course, Arthur Matlock. He has a room upstairs!"

"And most likely some peephole so he can look down and see where the *Dorset* is going—or he has the house bugged for sound. Then he makes his map and drops it in the bust of Morgan on his way to his workshop. The road goes right by the manor."

"It is a beautiful plan," Fil said. "Then whoever is doing the smuggling takes the map from the bust and knows where *not* to go. As long as the smugglers know where the *Dorset* will be, they can avoid her and get their goods on the coast with little difficulty."

"That's got to be the way it was worked. But tonight Reggie spoiled their plans by picking up all the busts of Morgan. When they were bronzed the villains didn't know which one contained the map."

"And that's why Morgan in his ghostly costume was up here smashing them. He had to get that information."

Filbert suddenly looked puzzled. "But, Herb, he didn't get it. You just found the paper when you smashed the bust yourself."

"That's right. And that's why they had to use the boat and the river to go by Matlock's place and get the information. It undoubtedly slowed them down."

Fil was thoughtful. "Last night I had the impression that Phoebe was bellowing a lot longer than usual. The horrible noise was simply designed to disguise some other noise, wasn't it? But what made you suspect?"

"Ramón's phone call just now. He took a quick look at Matlock's engine on his way out of here last night."

"And?"

"He checked it over before Matlock got there and he just told me its *sole* purpose is to *make noise,* as you have already figured out. Ramón said any engineer could have spotted it for a phony."

Parkhurst made a sudden, soundless appearance. "Sir, a Mr. Cravatt to see you."

"Cravatt?"

"He's the fellow we met at Mr. Sage's shop, you remember, the one who was interested in your old swords and things."

"But I told him I wasn't prepared to sell," Fil answered, very annoyed. "Let's go down and see what he wants."

Reggie followed us downstairs to meet Mr. Cravatt.

I don't know where Parkhurst had put the fellow, because when we went into the Great Room, it was empty. Then the door opened and in came the mousy man with a series of running bows.

"So sorry to trouble you," he began in a voice as gooey as his smile. "I was in the area and thought it might be an expeditious time to examine your collection."

"But I thought I made it quite clear that the armor and weapons in the manor belong to my father. I am in no position to sell them."

The gooey smile got gooier. "Certainly, I understand, Mr. Golightly, but surely it will not harm anything if I examine them. Now, will it?"

"Oh, bother!" Fil sank down in his fluffy chair.

Reggie called to Parkhurst who was stationed at the door like one of the suits of armor that were scattered about the manor. "Parkhurst, would you be a good fellow and bring us some tea?"

Parkhurst checked with Fil, who nodded, and then slipped silently from the room.

Cravatt's eyes fell upon the sword over the fireplace and he came to life.

"Verry good. Verry good, indeed. What a marvelous sword!" Then he realized that he looked a little too enthusiastic for a buyer and frowned and shook his head.

At first Fil was annoyed at the presence of the oily man, but now his curiosity was aroused. "Can you quote a price, Mr. Cravatt?"

The dealer's face contorted as if thinking gave him a headache. His shoulders danced a dramatic shrug. "Without a careful inspection it is difficult to say. However, I would estimate that . . . perhaps seven or eight hundred pounds."

"I have had it appraised for a good deal more than that," Fil lied.

Cravatt's face became the biggest artificial smile I've ever seen. His hands went out in a why-don't-we-talk-this-thing-over gesture, and he was absolutely stunned to discover that one hand now held a full tea cup as he brought it back to his body. Parkhurst had done his work. Cravatt sipped his tea, using the time to sharpen his already very sharp bargaining abilities. "Please understand, the price I mentioned was only a preliminary figure."

I watched Cravatt finish his tea in one big gulp just as Parkhurst was passing tea cups to Reggie, Fil and myself.

A second later, Cravatt groaned, and slumped forward in his chair.

"Good gracious, he's dead!" Reggie yelled.

I went over and studied Cravatt's face. "He's out, but he's not dead."

We all looked at Parkhurst at once. He understood and apologized. "I left the tea for just a moment, sir, while I went for sugar. It appears that someone has altered it."

This was his way of saying that while he was out of the kitchen for that minute someone dropped a *whammy* into the tea. While I was sure that Cravatt wasn't really in danger, there was no point taking chances. I'm not an expert on knockout drops. "We'd better get him to the doctor."

"I'll take him straightaway," Fil said.

I stopped him. "Do you think Reggie is well enough to do it?"

"I'll be happy to, Herb. I feel fine," Reggie answered, pushing his tea cup away from him.

Reggie left the room with surprising speed and by the time Fil and I carried the unconscious Mr. Cravatt outside, he was waiting at the front door in an ancient car.

Fil turned to me as the car moved away toward the road. "Why didn't you want me to go, Herb?"

"Reggie can get Cravatt to the doctor's without our help. Besides, if you leave, there's no blood relative around to look after Morgan's sword."

"You are pulling my leg again."

"What I'm trying to say, Fil, is that I don't think Cravatt is in any real danger. The people involved in this smuggling operation are not killers, at least not so far. They didn't even kill Beowolf, did they?"

"Then why did they drug Cravatt?"

"They couldn't have known Cravatt would drink his tea before us. They may have intended all of us to get it—or to get the rest of us out of the manor. Because I'll wager my best Sunday tomahawk against three suits of your moldy armor that tonight's the night there's going to be a lot of action in the depths beneath Sudbury Hall."

"For the first time I agree wholeheartedly with you, Herb."

"There's no point in us staying out here any longer beating our gums. Let's go. I think it's about time we shook out your ghost."

13

But I'm Nonviolent!

When we entered the house again, my body was stiff. That rain had gotten to me; I had rusted. Needed oil in the worst way. It took great effort to force myself back into the Great Room. Nor was Fil exactly chipper.

It was fear. We were scared right down to our toes. It took a while to disengage my tongue.

Finally I said, "Why don't we have a look around, Fil? Maybe we'll stumble across something."

Fil was having the same trouble with his tongue. "Do you—do you think that's wise? Whoever wanted us to leave now knows that we didn't."

"Good point."

We stayed where we were, wondering what to do next and not too thrilled about that nagging feeling that we had to do something. The Great Room, for all its faults, was comparatively safe. The rest of the house was enemy territory. Fil begin playing aimless chords on the piano. I ignored him, trying to come up with some brilliant—but safe—solution. How to find out what was going on at Sudbury Hall without getting killed in the process?

Then the piano gave me an idea—not a brilliant one, I admit, but at least it had possibilities. My eyes moved from Fil to the tape recorder beside him which he had told me he used to record his practice sessions so that he could detect his mistakes.

"What's on that tape now, Fil?"

My question threw him for the moment. He screwed up his eyes in thought. "Just the last section of Ravel's 'Bolero,' I think. Why?"

"It's only an idea. If we turn it on kind of loud, maybe it'll give the impression we're still in here. Then we can move around without worrying as much about someone surprising us."

His look was doubtful. "I suppose that's sensible. Okay, I'll turn it on."

I took the precaution of picking up a candle as we left the room, with the "Bolero" picking up steam behind us. I stopped to listen. "Hey, you're getting better, Fil."

"Thank you," he answered unenthusiastically. His mind was on other things. "Where shall we start?"

"How about where we first saw Uncle Morgan?"

When we reached the hallway where Morgan had first appeared, I lit the candle and carefully moved alongside the paneling. Although there were electric lights spaced along the hall, they were weak and too far apart to help much. Together Fil and I felt over the paneling with no success.

"Do you really think he came out here, Herb?"

"Had to. He suddenly appeared in the middle of this hallway, didn't he? There aren't any doorways around here, so he had to come out of the wall. Keep tapping."

Fil shrugged, but went ahead looking and tapping his way along the dark paneling.

And then, just like that, he got a hollow answer to his knock. "I may have come upon something, old fellow," he said lightly. He tapped again. Another hollow reply.

We both worked on that panel, pushing, shoving, tapping, and when my hand hit the beak of a carved eagle in the woodwork, the wall moved. A panel swung open and I thought I would faint.

I didn't, but I confess that I was scared to death when I stepped into that hole. There were no big smiles on Fil's face as he followed me in, either.

The smell was enough to turn a strong man's stomach; damp, rank, and putrid, like a dishcloth that had been left in a soggy heap. We went down a flight of stairs; the walls changed to slimy rock, cold and sweaty.

"Where do you think we're going?" Fil whispered so softly I could hardly hear him.

"I've got the discouraging feeling we're headed straight for that Small Room your Uncle Morgan talked about. Friend, this may be bad."

"Yes, it may be sticky, but let's get on with it."

We got on with it, going down deeper into the earth. The candle was our only light. It was comforting, but not all that much.

After turning and twisting, Fil asked, "Do you know what direction we're going in?"

"Nope," I answered, inching my way forward in a creepy criss-cross of cobwebs. "Yichhh!"

My smeller told me we were getting closer to the river. I moved as quietly as I could. Fil, too. My throat was sandpaper, and the slimy green stuff swooshing against my face made me feel sick. I didn't get sick, although I can't remember breathing too much, either.

Somebody was up ahead. I could hear him working, as

if maybe he was pulling things around. Then we heard the murmur of voices.

The candle had to be blown out. We weren't going to surprise anyone if we were lit up like a Christmas tree. It was one of the biggest battles of my life with myself. Fil suddenly reached around and huffed it out.

Man, it was dark.

I felt my way forward with Fil's breath on my neck. I remember suddenly telling myself, "Herbert García, your mother would never approve of this." Boy, would she give me a clout!

We kept easing forward.

I could tell we were getting closer to the river; I could hear the distant sound of rushing water, and the thumping sound of something just ahead got louder. *Thump. Thump. Thump.*

It was a good thing, too, because our knees were making a pretty good racket as they knocked against each other. A light flickered ahead.

I turned the corner and there he was.

Arthur Matlock.

We both stared, stunned, into each other's eyes. His were blue, and blank with surprise.

"I'm nonviolent," I told him, and watched in shock as his expression turned to a snarl.

Please don't think that I'm showing off or anything when I tell you that the dive I took at his feet was magnificent. It was one of my best—graceful, shoulders angled, chin tucked in, and just the right height off the ground.

Unfortunately, I don't remember making contact. I got clobbered. The room exploded with stars, like a cloudless desert night.

Dimly, I heard a voice full of horror shout, *"For God's*

sake, don't hit him again, Matlock!" Wing Commander Selkirk's voice.

Then I heard a lot of scuffling, Fil's grunt, feet running. I got groggily to my own feet.

We were in a small room carved out of rock. Boxes everywhere. I saw three men jump into a small boat. They heaved the boxes overboard in their frantic rush, and struggled to start the motor.

My head was clear now. Fil lay stunned on the cave floor, shaking his head.

The men pushed the boat out. The motor started and coughed.

Without thinking, I kicked off my mocassins, stripped my jacket, and dove in after them.

Wow! Nobody told me how cold English rivers are in the summer!

With steady strokes, I swam toward the boat. It had drifted into the river now, and the motor revved again and then started with a roar downriver.

I swam a few yards after them, the current catching me. It was no use. I couldn't catch them now, and it had been stupid to try. My bones were freezing. I turned back.

But now something very odd happened. My limbs seemed to be disconnected from the rest of my body. First they went cold, then beyond cold, then numb. I could scarcely feel them. And the river current was so much stronger than it had seemed to be. It was carrying me along, pushing me up, pulling me down.

I panicked, thrashing wildly, terror pumping strength into dead arms and legs.

I was drowning!

Dimly, I heard another motor roar to life downstream, and heard a distant shout.

I could not see—I knew that, but I was seeing clearly, inside my head, somehow. I saw my mother, her plump face benign; I saw my father, solid as a rock, his face steady and sure; and I saw Ramón. Ramón, the emotionless, one eyebrow half-cocked.

A voice called, "Herb! Brother!"

Water filled my lungs. I felt life ebbing from me, but I was not afraid.

14

"Not to Worry, Herb."

The water was choking me. I gagged. Someone was forcing air down my lungs. In. Out. In. Out.

I coughed. Someone said, "Thank God!"

My lungs were in a spasm. I coughed again and again. Then someone gently raised me up. I opened my eyes, and looked into the face of my brother Ramón.

But something was wrong; it didn't look like Ramón. Tears were streaming down his face and splattering onto mine.

"Hey, whassamatter you?" I smiled unevenly. "You trying to drown me again?" I went into another coughing fit.

Ramón thumped me on the back. "Didn't I tell you to be careful? Didn't I tell you?"

Another figure loomed beside us in the darkness—Ben Richmond, the writer I knew to be a phony. "Look out!" I yelled at Ramón.

"It's all right," Ramón said. "Richmond, he's going to be fine. You'd better hightail it down to the beach. Wakefield's going to need help, and I'll be right behind you."

As Richmond left, and before I could wonder what he

138

had been doing there, Fil came staggering through the trees. "You beat the curse! You came through the shadow of death!" he gasped.

"Take care of this wet cub for me," Ramón told him. He turned to me and ordered, "Listen, kid, you two go on up to the house. I'm going down to the beach to give Inspector Wakefield a hand. You hear?"

"Sure, Ramón," I said. Ramón faded into the trees downriver.

Fil helped me up. "How do you feel, Herb? Come on, I'll help you to the house."

"I'm all right," I insisted. "What about you? You didn't look too great the last time I saw you in the Small Room."

"I'm a bit woozy, but I'll be all right."

"Fil? You really want to go up to the house? Do you feel like sneaking down to the beach to see what's going on?"

Fil was tempted, but he said, "We'd better get you to bed. You're half frozen."

"No, really, I'm okay now. Come on, let's hit the beach," I said, and laughed.

"I knew it. You're getting giddy. No, I'd like to as much as you, Herb, but you may go into shock or something. I don't want to lose you to the curse, after all."

Grumbling, I started back toward the Hall, Fil helping me along. "You know," I said, "I owe Wing Commander Selkirk something, even if he did turn out to be a crook. If he hadn't yelled at Matlock when he did, I think Matlock might have really clobbered me good."

I could feel Fil stare at me accusingly. "You knew the Wing Commander was in on it all along, didn't you?"

"He was my number one suspect, I'll admit. For several reasons. Once we had seen Matlock in his lab just after we'd seen the ghost, I felt sure the ghost had been Selkirk. He was the only other local who was tall enough to play Uncle Morgan.

"Too, an old airman like Selkirk surely would have spotted Matlock's engine for a phony that could do nothing but make noise.

"And remember when we went to the Wing Commander's house after the *Dorset* was set afire? He was bandaging up his hand and said he'd hurt it on the thorns from his rose bushes. But I caught a glimpse of the wound and it looked more like a burn to me."

"I just hate to believe it, that's all," Fil said.

"But even before those things happened, Fil . . . well, look. What was the first really strange thing that happened at Sudbury Hall, even before I got here?"

"I saw the ghost, and Miss Stokes vanished."

"And whose friend was Miss Stokes?"

"Wing Commander Selkirk's, of course. She was supposed to be his house guest, and then I offered to put her up here because he didn't have room in his small cottage— oh. I see. She was more connected with him than with anyone else. But why was it necessary for her to disappear?"

I was starting to shiver. "I can't figure that one for sure. I hate to think that Selkirk might have—harmed her. We'll just have to wait to find out, I guess." Chills were beginning to grip my body. Fil noticed at once, took off his sweater and shirt to bundle me with, and hurriedly helped me back to the Great Room.

I collapsed onto a sofa and shivered at last in peace, wrapped around with blankets by a concerned Filbert. Parkhurst appeared as if on cue with hot water bottles and tea. It was a pleasure to see him. The tea was hot and strong, and oddly comforting. For the first time, I began to feel like a real Englishman.

When I awoke some two hours later, Ramón and Fil were sitting across from me.

I stretched luxuriously and said, "Hi. You get them all?"

"All of them at this end of the smuggling scheme. Selkirk really took it hard."

Fil brought me another cup of tea, and as I sipped it I asked Ramón, "Did Selkirk say what happened to Miss Stokes?"

"No, but Inspector Wakefield's men had already found out about that yesterday. That's what made Wakefield decide to close in last night.

"Miss Stokes was in love with Selkirk—yes, Herb, I see what you're thinking, but even old people fall in love. Miss Stokes was in love with Wing Commander Selkirk. What I think happened was this. She heard the horn, went out to investigate, saw the ghost again—you remember she had seen it with me earlier that evening—and suspected who it was. When she confronted Selkirk with her suspicions later that night, he blurted out the whole thing. Miss Stokes couldn't forgive dishonesty, but she couldn't bring herself to tattle on him to the police, either. So she took the easy way out and flew to Italy. She's been there ever since, safe and sound.

"Selkirk himself didn't know what had happened to her, and the guy almost collapsed with relief when he heard she was okay."

"I can't help but feel sorry for him," Fil said. "What do you suppose made an honorable man like that get involved in such a thing? Money?"

I hazarded a guess. "I'll bet the money was the least of it. I don't think he thought of this himself, do you? After all, the smugglers had to have a flier. I bet they got him into this in the beginning more to satisfy his longing to fly again than for anything else. It may have seemed a harmless sort of adventure the first time, and then he got in too deep to get out again. They may have blackmailed him."

"Hey, hold on! What's this *fly* business? You mean they smuggled the stuff in by air, after all?"

I looked at Ramón, and he nodded. "Go on," he told me, "you're doing fine."

"They used an amphibian, didn't they?" I asked. Ramón nodded again. "A flying boat, as Selkirk called it. Remember, he said he flew one during the Second World War? He also flew it in this area, so he, better than most, would know every inch of the coastline. And Matlock made Phoebe shriek to cover the noise of his take-offs and landings."

"You know," Fil said, "I thought of that and then dismissed it as ridiculous. I remember now, though, that Selkirk was looking at weather charts when we visited his cottage."

"You can't fly if you don't know the weather," I said. "The amphibian would be perfect. They could put it down someplace far away from the shore and from the *Dorset,* and then taxi up to the river. Then they could unload their cargo onto the boat and bring it into the Small Room until they were ready to take it on to London or wherever. It must have put a big crimp in their style when your family moved in here."

"Hey! That boathouse we looked at, the one with the big padlock on the door near the Wing Commander's cottage! Is that—?"

"I'll bet my bear-claw necklace that's where they found the amphibian. How about it, Ramón?"

"True," he smiled.

"Fil, remember the tracks leading from the boathouse to the water?"

"Yes, I thought they were made by a boat trailer."

"Too wide for that. But just about right for amphibian wheels."

Parkhurst glided in with hot scones (biscuits to us), butter, and jam. I popped one into my mouth, and my happiness was complete. They weren't Mama's *tamales*, but they would do.

Buttering a scone carefully, Fil asked, "Do I have it straight? Selkirk was more or less responsible for Miss Stokes's disappearance; he was the one who masqueraded as Uncle Morgan's ghost; and he did the flying to smuggle in the booty. My word, they really kept the old boy hopping, didn't they? Was that all he did?"

"Well," I began, and glanced again at Ramón, who closed his eyes and nodded. "Well, I'm afraid he was the one who set fire to the *Dorset,* too."

"You must be right, even though I thought Ben Richmond said Agatha Howe did that."

"No, I think the poor old Wing Commander was dressing up again. If it wasn't Agatha, it had to be someone at least her height, and Selkirk fills the bill. And I don't think it was Agatha, because Agatha passed us in a car, waving cheerfully, just after we'd seen a person we thought to be her in the woods, remember? Richmond didn't exactly say he saw Agatha; he said he saw someone dressed in a brown coat and red kerchief similar to the outfit Agatha always wears."

"Then it wasn't our Agatha!" Fil crowed.

I gave him the fish-eye. He sounded so delighted to think that Agatha Howe was innocent. I couldn't believe it! By

the beardless face of my grandfather, the guy had a crush
on her! I shook my head. There's no figuring people. Black
Dan and Uncle Morgan might get together after all, in a
manner of speaking!

I turned toward Ramón. "The only one I couldn't figure
was Ben Richmond. I knew he wasn't a writer like he
claimed to be, but I wasn't sure just what he was."

"He was working with Inspector Wakefield," Ramón said.
"He's with customs. And part of his assignment was trying
to keep you two in sight."

"I wonder how long customs has been onto them?" I
pondered, taking another scone and watching the butter
melt into it.

"You keep saying *them*," said Filbert. "Just whom do
you mean by *them*, if Ben Richmond wasn't in on it? I
couldn't see a thing down in the Small Room."

"I mean the Wing Commander, Arthur Matlock, and
Mr. Sage."

"Mr. Sage! Oh, come now, Herb! Surely not! His family
has been respected here for generations!"

"Sorry about that, Fil, but he's bound to have been in
on it. After all, he almost has to be the one who set up the
legend about the horn sounding and the ghost walking. And
who had a better chance to find out about the Small Room?
And the compartment in the bust of Uncle Morgan, where
Matlock left his maps of the *Dorset*'s movements? Sage had
control of this place while it was empty. And I'll bet it was
he who forged those documents by Edmund, Sixth Earl of
Sudbury, to make us believe the legend was true. It was
really clever of him, too, forging two different things like
that. If anyone checked one against the other, they'd be
doubly convinced they were genuine. No, I'll wager our
respectable Mr. Sage masterminded this whole affair."

"So Selkirk claims," Ramón put in.

Fil allowed his unpleasant surprise to disturb his appetite for only a moment. Then he reached for another scone and handed the tray to Ramón, who helped himself. "It grieves me to agree that it's only too logical," Fil mourned. "It's true, Mr. Sage was Johnny-on-the-spot. And there's been a lot of traffic on the way to his office of late."

Parkhurst brought in another tray of sandwiches and pastries, and we settled down to letting our appetites run wild.

A thought struck me. "Ramón?"

"Tell me."

"What about Beowolf?"

"Ah, Beowolf. They had to get rid of him. He was sniffing around and barking at them too much. At first they kept him in the boathouse, muzzled, but after he got loose and started barking, they drugged him and took him along on a smuggling run to Portsmouth, and dumped him along the way."

"How about the antique dealer, Cravatt? Was he in it?"

"No evidence of that so far. Sage probably built up his interest to keep your attention away from what was really going on here."

Fil moved to his piano and played a sprightly tune, happier than I'd seen him since I arrived.

Me, I was thinking of my own personal mystery. "Hey, Ramón," I said at last. "How come you knew Inspector Wakefield well enough that he'd let you in on all this?"

Ramón grunted softly. "I told you. Once I worked with him, when our interests happened to be the same."

"Yes, but, Ramón—"

Ramón stood and stretched. "It's time for me to get going. Good luck to you, Fil. Take care of this one for me, okay?" To me, Ramón said, "I may not see you again for quite a time. Take care, eh? Or I'll write Mama."

"Listen, Ramón, great stone face that you are—" I stopped suddenly, remembering Ramón's face, tears streaking down it, as I lay on the beach.

I shook myself and went on. "You can't bluff me. You probably won't write home for six months."

Ramón looked pained. He held his hand out to me and grinned. I held back in the old way, but then the dam broke and I threw my arms around him in a bear hug. "Good luck, big brother. Don't take any wooden nickels, you hear? Go with God."

"No wooden nickels," he promised, and then he was gone. I heard the door close, and felt the familiar tightening in my stomach.

"Go with God, Ramón," I whispered.

Fil put a hand on my shoulder. "Not to worry, Herb. He can take good care of himself." I nodded. "I say, even with that rather lengthy explanation, it still doesn't explain how Morgan could just disappear in this room while I fumbled for the light."

"Well, we checked the walls, but there's one place we didn't check."

"The fireplace? A fire was going in there. The ceiling? Ah, the floor!"

"I'll wager there's a trap door leading down into the passageway under the house." We looked at each other. Neither rose to the challenge. "Let's leave that one to check out later."

Fil began to play again. "I feel a proper fool! I was so sure that Morgan was actually walking these halls."

"Maybe he was, Filbert ol' buddy. Maybe he was. For all I know, Black Dan is hanging around, too."

Well, I had my trip to Europe, and as far as Cousin Philip and Cousin Flora, my two wiseacre relatives from Albuquerque, are concerned, it didn't do me a lick of good. I still haven't marched along the Champs Élysées, or fallen overboard in the Grand Canal.

Shortly after I dragged my tired body back to Pueblo, New Mexico, I had a nice letter from Fil. The Wing Commander, Matlock, Sage, and their far-flung accomplices were all in custody. Beowolf was back, and Reggie was painting again, mostly ghosts. He was also growing his hair back and seemed to be in happy touch with the next world as often as with this. They had found the trap door in the Great Room and were having a fine time with it.

For Fil, the mystery was solved. For me, it wasn't. To this day, I still don't know if Parkhurst is a first or a last name.

As far as Sudbury Hall is concerned, Fil wrote, there are no more smugglers—at least no more live ones.

It's a funny thing, though; he wrote that Beowolf refuses to walk along the upstairs hallway. Cringes, in fact, if anyone suggests it. And Fil went on to write that soon after I left he and Reggie were going along a corridor on the third floor when they ran into a friend.

That's right. Morgan, Fourth Earl of Sudbury. He just sort of appeared like a mist of fog. But he was smiling, and he gave them a sweeping bow before he melted away. Quite an amiable chap, after all.

Now that I've told you this tale, I'm going to ask you to do one thing for me. If you meet Cousins Philip and Flora, for gosh sake don't tell them about it. If they knew I had an adventure like that, they'd be pestering the dickens out of me to take another trip across the Atlantic to get some culture.

Frankly, my head couldn't take it.